175 Easy-to-Do
VALENTINE
CRAFTS

CREATIVE USES · FOR RECYCLABLES

Edited by Sharon Dunn Umnik

BOYDS MILLS PRESS

Inside this book...

you'll find a fabulous assortment of crafts made from recyclable items and inexpensive things found in or around your house. Have pencils, crayons, scissors, tape, paintbrushes, and other supplies for craft making close by. —*the Editor*

Copyright © 2001 by Boyds Mills Press
All rights reserved

Published by Bell Books
Boyds Mills Press, Inc.
A Highlights Company
815 Church Street
Honesdale, Pennsylvania 18431
Printed in China

U.S. Cataloging-in-Publication Data
      (Library of Congress Standards)

175 easy-to-do valentine crafts : creative uses for recyclables / edited
by Sharon Dunn Umnik.—1st ed.
[64] p. : col. ill. ;   cm.
Includes index.
Summary: Includes step-by-step directions to make decorations,
gifts, and greeting cards for Valentine's Day.
ISBN 1-56397-672-2
1. Valentine decorations. 2. Handicraft. 3. Recycling (Waste, etc.).
I. Umnik, Sharon Dunn. II. Title.
745.594/ 1 21 2001   CIP   AC
00-109926

First edition, 2001
Book designed by Charlie Cary
The text of this book is set in 11-point New Century Schoolbook.

Visit our Web site at www.boydsmillspress.com

10 9 8 7 6 5 4 3 2 1

Craft Contributors: Patricia Barley, Frances Benson, Linda Bloomgren, Deborah Bowen,
Beverly Swerdlow Brown, Judy Burke, Martha Carpenter, Karen Lee Davidow, B. J. Deike,
Ruth Dougherty, Jean E. Doyle, Doris D. Engles, Anita Fitz-Gerald, Clara Flammang,
Tanya Turner Fry, Elsa Garratt, Isabel Joshlin Glaser, Nora Grubmeyer, Janice Hauter,
Juanita Havill, Loretta Holz, Marjorie Homonoff, Carmen Horn, Ellen Javernick, Helen Jeffries,
Jacqueline Koury, Twilla Lamm, Ella L. Langenberg, Lee Lindeman, Miriam Twyman Lister,
M. Mable Lunz, Clare Mishica, June Rose Mobly, Dorice Moore, Miranda Murphy, Anita Page,
Evelyne Good Pearson, Beatrice Bachrach Perri, James W. Perrin, Jr., Dora M. Prado,
Erma Reynolds, Joyce Rinehart, Kathy Ross, Audrey A. Scannell, Jane Scherer, Barbara J. Smith,
Sylvia W. Sproat, Margaret Squires, Sally E. Stuart, June Swanson, Helen A. Thomas,
Sharon Dunn Umnik, Jan M. Van Pelt, Jean Vetter, Agnes Choate Wonson, Patsy N. Zimmerman.

Valentine Holders

The custom of exchanging greeting cards called valentines with sweethearts, friends, and family members may have begun as early as the 1400s. Place the valentines you receive in one of these special holders.

PAPER-PLATE HOLDER
(two heavy paper plates, thick yarn, construction paper)

1. Cut a small section from two heavy paper plates.

2. Glue the paper plates together rim to rim with the bottoms facing out. Leave the cut section open for a pocket.

3. Cut a long piece of thick yarn for a hanger and glue it around the outer edges of the plates. Knot the yarn ends together at the bottom. Glue other yarn pieces around the top of the pocket.

4. Decorate the front of the holder with hearts cut from construction paper. Hang the holder on a doorknob.

PAPER-BAG HOLDER
(lunch bag, cardboard, construction paper)

1. Fold down the top of a lunch bag about 1 to 2 inches. Write your name across the folded top.

2. Cut out a piece of cardboard to fit in the bottom of the bag to help it stand.

3. Draw and cut out a heart shape from construction paper. Glue it to the front of the bag.

MAIL-TRUCK HOLDER
(construction paper, yarn)

1. Fold a sheet of white construction paper in half lengthwise, keeping the fold at the bottom.

2. Cut a section from the top right corner to make the truck shape. Glue a piece of blue paper even with the fold on the white paper, making the bottom of the truck. Add a red stripe in the middle. Cut out and glue on red paper circles for wheels.

3. Write "U.S. Mail" on the white portion of the truck. Glue on paper hearts. Staple the edges of the truck, leaving the top of the truck open.

4. Using a paper punch, punch a hole at the front and back of the truck. Tie a piece of yarn for a hanger.

"KNOTS ABOUT YOU" WREATH
(plastic-foam tray, fabric, lace)

1. To make the wreath base, cut out a large heart from a plastic-foam tray. Draw a smaller heart inside the large heart. Cut out the center heart.

2. Cut fabric into strips about 1/2 inch wide and 5 inches long. Tie each strip in a half-knot around the heart-shaped wreath base until it is covered.

3. Wrap a piece of lace around your hand four times, slide it off, and tie another piece of lace around the center of the wrapped lace to make a bow. Glue the bow to the wreath.

4. Glue a piece of lace to the back of the wreath for a hanger.

VALENTINE MOUSE CARD
(construction paper)

1. Fold a large sheet of construction paper in half. Cut out a large half-heart shape from one side of the folded paper.

2. With the heart folded, glue on a heart-shaped paper ear, nose, and eye. Add whiskers and a tail.

3. Write a greeting inside.

SWEETHEART HAT
(poster board, paper, glitter, paper doily)

1. Cut a large heart from red poster board. Draw a small heart in the center of the large heart and cut it out.

2. Glue white paper to the back of the cutout heart section. Turn the heart right side up and draw a letter on the white heart with glue. Sprinkle it with glitter and let dry.

3. Glue the heart to a round paper doily. Cut a strip of white poster board and glue the doily and the heart to the center of the strip. Staple the ends of the strip together so that it fits around your head.

KEY CHAIN
(plastic lid, felt, metal book ring)

1. Cut away the rim from a small plastic lid.

2. Cut two circles of felt to fit the center of the lid. Glue one piece of felt to each side of the lid.

3. Draw and cut out hearts from another color of felt and glue to the center.

4. Using a paper punch, punch a hole near the edge. Attach a metal book ring through the hole. Keys can be attached to the ring.

SWEET-SMELLING VALENTINES
(felt, fabric, lace, cotton balls, dried herbs or flowers, yarn)

1. Cut out two identical shapes from a piece of felt. Glue them together at the edges, leaving an opening at the top.

2. Decorate with pieces of fabric and lace. Fill with cotton balls and a dried herb or flower, such as mint or lavender. Glue shut.

3. Glue yarn around the edges, leaving a loop for a hanger.

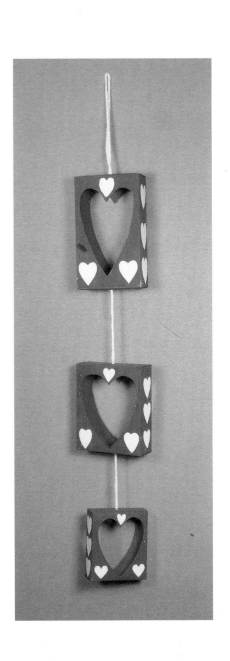

VALENTINE MOBILE
(three different-sized cardboard boxes, poster paint, paper, yarn)

1. Collect three different-sized cardboard boxes. Draw and cut out hearts from each large side of the boxes.

2. Cover the boxes with red poster paint. Let dry. Decorate them with white paper hearts.

3. Poke a small hole in the top and bottom of each box. Place white yarn through the holes and make knots, tying the boxes together.

4. Tie a loop at the top for a hanger.

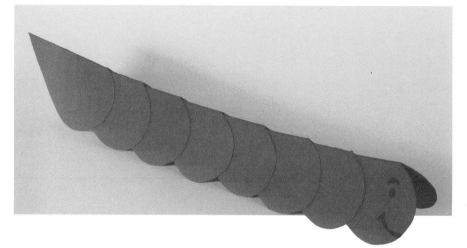

WORM CARD
(construction paper)

1. Cut out eight identical red hearts from construction paper. Fold each heart in half. Glue them on top of each other, overlapping them a bit.

2. Draw an eye and a mouth with a marker. Open the worm and write "I'd like to worm my way into your heart."

SWEETHEART BASKET
(tissue paper, plastic berry basket, chenille sticks, paper doilies, ribbon)

1. Tape red tissue paper onto the outside of a plastic berry basket.

2. To make the handle, twist two chenille sticks together and poke the ends through each side of the basket. Twist the ends of the chenille sticks, attaching them to the basket.

3. Decorate the basket with sections cut from paper doilies and ribbons.

4. Fill the basket with snacks.

SEWING NEEDLE CASE
(paper, felt, ribbon)

1. On a 3 1/2-inch square piece of paper, draw and cut out a heart.

2. Cut a piece of felt 3 1/2 inches by 7 inches. Fold it in half with the short sides together.

3. Pin the paper heart on the felt so the left edge of the heart overlaps the fold about 1/4 inch. Trace around the heart with a pencil. With the felt folded, cut along the pencil line, leaving the hearts connected by the fold as shown.

4. Decorate the heart with ribbon. Store sewing needles and safety pins inside.

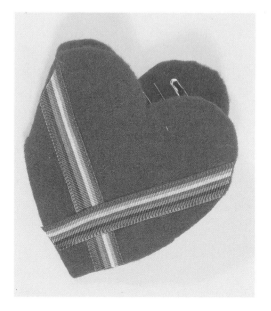

SPINNING HEARTS
(paint stir stick, acrylic paint, construction paper, thumbtack, bead)

1. Cover a paint stir stick with acrylic paint and let dry. Cut out small paper hearts and glue them along the stick.

2. Cut out a 9-inch square piece of paper. Draw a diagonal line from each corner as shown.
Cut a 4-inch slit from the corner toward the center on each diagonal line.

3. Punch a small hole at the edge of each of the left-hand angles of the four triangles. Working clockwise, lift and pull the corner of each punched triangle toward the center of the square.

4. Insert a thumbtack through the holes, the center of the square, and a small bead. Push the thumbtack into the paint stir stick. Glue on paper hearts.

VALENTINE RING
(two paper plates, paper, string)

1. Cut the centers out of two paper plates. Using red paper, cut a heart shape that will fit in the center of the plate rims.

2. Tie a long string to the heart and glue the two plates rim to rim, with the string between them. Use the extra string for a hanger.

3. Decorate with markers and cut-paper letters and hearts.

VALENTINE TIC-TAC-TOE
(cardboard, paint, paper, yarn, ten plastic caps)

1. Cut a square piece of cardboard and cover it with paint. When dry, glue a large paper heart in the center.

2. Glue on pieces of yarn to form the lines of the playing board.

3. Gather ten plastic caps. Cut out five pink paper hearts and five red paper hearts. Glue one heart on top of each cap.

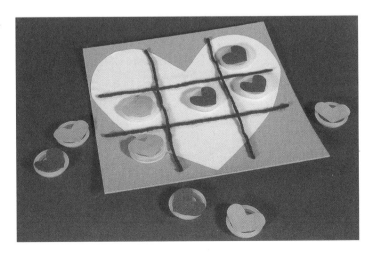

"BEE" MINE, VALENTINE
(cardboard egg carton, yarn, chenille sticks,
waxed paper, paper, cardboard)

1. Cut out one cup section from a cardboard egg carton. Cover it with glue and wind brown yarn around it to look like a beehive.

2. Wrap a yellow chenille stick around your finger to make the body of a bee. Wrap a shorter piece of black chenille stick around the bee to make stripes. Glue the bee to the hive. Cut wings from waxed paper and eyes from paper. Glue them to the bee.

3. Draw and cut out a large heart shape from cardboard. Cover it with paper. Glue the hive to the center of the heart.

4. Write the message "Will you (bee) mine, Valentine?"

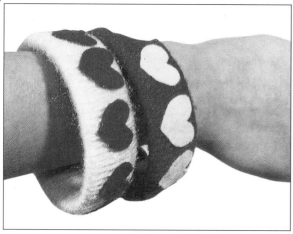

VALENTINE BRACELETS
(plastic-foam cups, yarn, felt)

1. Draw a line about 1 inch down from the top edge of two plastic-foam cups. Cut around the cups on the lines, making the bracelet forms.

2. Wrap pink or red yarn around each bracelet. Glue the ends to the inside of the bracelet.

3. Decorate the bracelets by gluing on hearts cut from pink, red, or white felt.

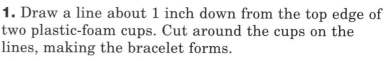

SURPRISE VALENTINE TUBE
(paper towel tube, yarn, red tissue paper, aluminum foil,
paper, snack food)

1. Cut a section from a paper towel tube to make it a little shorter. For a hanger, tape the ends of a piece of yarn to the inside of each tube end.

2. Cut and glue a folded strip of red tissue paper around the edge of each end of the tube. Cut slits in the tissue for fringe.

3. Cover the tube with glue and aluminum foil. Glue on cut-paper hearts. Place bite-sized snacks inside the tube. Stuff the tube ends with crumpled tissue paper.

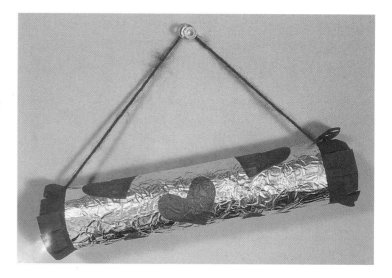

PEANUT VALENTINE
(construction paper)

1. Fold a piece of light-brown construction paper in half. Draw the shape of a large peanut, with one side of the peanut on the fold.

2. Cut out the peanut along the dotted line, being careful not to cut the fold as shown. Decorate the peanut with black dots.

3. Inside write "I'm nuts about you, Valentine!"

PLANTER OF LOVE
(clay flowerpot and base; acrylic paint; paper; high-gloss, water-based crystal-clear glaze)

1. To decorate a plain clay flowerpot and base, cover them with white acrylic paint. Let dry overnight.

2. Cut a heart-shaped pattern from paper. With a pencil, lightly trace around the heart on the pot, making a design. Paint the hearts, adding other details with paint. Let dry.

3. To protect the clay pot, *ask an adult to help you* cover it with a clear glaze, following the package directions.

VALENTINE WAND
(paper, paper doily, wooden dowel, permanent marker, yarn)

1. Cut two hearts the same size from red paper. Glue a paper doily between the two hearts. Insert a wooden dowel between the two hearts at the bottom before the glue dries.

2. Color the stick with a red permanent marker.

3. Decorate the wand with more hearts and a yarn bow.

PATCHWORK CARD
(construction paper, fabric)

1. For the card, fold a piece of construction paper in half. Fold it over in half again the other way. Then unfold the card. Draw a heart in the lower right-hand square. Cut out the heart.

2. Fold the paper together so the heart opening is on the top layer and the fold is on the left. With a pencil, trace through the heart shape onto the square beneath.

3. Unfold the card again and glue on small pieces of different-colored fabric, side by side, to fill the traced heart shape. Some fabric may extend beyond the shape.

4. Dot glue around the fabric heart edges. Refold the card, pressing the cutout section over the fabric heart.

5. Draw a border on the front of the card. Write a message inside.

"I LOVE YOU" BOOKMARK
(yarn, paper)

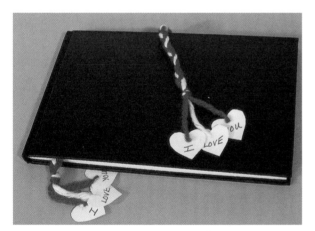

1. Cut three lengths of yarn—two of the same color and one of a different color—each about a foot long. Line up the pieces of yarn and tie them together into a knot about 1 inch from one end.

2. Braid by folding A over B and then C over A as shown in the diagram. Continue until the yarn is braided. Tie the strands into a knot again about 1 inch from the end.

3. Cut six small hearts from white paper. Write a three-word message on three hearts, writing one word on each heart. Write the same message or a different one on the other three hearts. Glue the hearts to the ends of the braid.

DOVE DOOR DECORATION
(construction paper, plastic-foam "peanuts," yarn)

1. Draw and cut out two doves from white construction paper. Glue them onto a large heart cut from pink paper.

2. Spread glue over the doves and press small plastic-foam "peanuts" into the glue. For the eyes, glue on black paper circles.

3. Cut out small hearts from red paper. Write valentine messages on them and glue them next to the doves' beaks.

4. For a hanger, thread a piece of yarn through two punched holes at the top of the decoration.

VALENTINE PALS
(old socks, cotton balls, thread, felt, construction paper)

1. Stuff an old clean sock as far as the heel with cotton balls. Twist the rest of the sock and wrap it with thread to make the tail.

2. Tie thread around other parts of the sock to shape a head and feet.

3. Cut ears and other heart-shaped features from felt or construction paper and glue them in place.

THE HEARTS GAME
(white poster board, permanent red marker, four plastic caps)

1. Draw four hearts of different sizes on a large piece of white poster board as shown. Add color with a permanent red marker.

2. Draw and cut out four small hearts from white poster board. Give each one a point value from 1 to 4. Glue one numbered heart to each heart on the board.

To play: Place the board on the floor. Players take turns tossing four plastic caps onto the board. The player with the highest number of points wins.

SENTIMENTAL SLATE
(four ice-cream sticks, yarn, black paper, white paint)

1. Form a square frame with four ice-cream sticks. Glue the sticks together at the corners and let dry.

2. Attach a piece of yarn to one stick for a hanger.

3. Cut a piece of black paper to fit the square frame, making a slate. Paint a message on the black paper using white paint. Let dry.

4. Glue the slate to the square frame.

TWIRLING HEART MOBILE
(paper, glitter, string, poster board)

1. Cut four strips of paper in different lengths and widths. Spread a thin layer of glue on one side of each strip. Sprinkle glitter on the glue. Let dry.

2. Fold each strip in half, with the glitter facing out. Curve the ends to form a heart shape. Spread glue on one outside end. Place a piece of string between the ends and glue them together.

3. Cut a large arrow from poster board. Add a piece of paper with a message. Tape the string ends to the back of the arrow, leaving the hearts hanging at different lengths and twirling in the air.

ROLL-A-HEART VALENTINE
(paper)

1. Cut a piece of paper in the shape of a heart.

2. Cut red and white paper into long narrow strips. Roll the strips around a pencil, glue the ends, and slide the rolls off the pencil.

3. Glue the white rolls around the edge of the heart. Then glue the red rolls inside the section of white rolls.

VALENTINE CARRIER
(construction paper, cereal box)

1. Glue red construction paper around the sides of a cereal box.

2. Fold a piece of paper in half, and cut a heart shape almost as wide as the box and about half as tall.

3. To make the handle, place the heart on the front of the box and trace around it with a pencil. Do the same on the back. Carefully cut out the area around the heart shapes as shown in the diagram. Cut a smaller heart out of the middle of both heart shapes.

4. Decorate the carrier with other hearts. Place your valentines inside, and hand them out to your family and friends.

FOUR-LEAF CLOVER VALENTINE
(thread spool, construction paper)

1. Cover a thread spool with glue and red construction paper. Cut four identical heart shapes from green paper. On one heart write "There's a secret message inside for you." Glue the hearts to the top of the spool to form a four-leaf clover.

2. Cut a long strip of paper the same width as the spool. Draw a heart and write a message or poem on it.

3. Roll the paper tightly and slip it into the hole in the bottom of the spool.

VALENTINE DANCER
(2-inch plastic-foam ball, plastic spice bottle, fabric, bottle cap, moveable plastic eyes, ribbon, chenille stick)

1. To make the head, use a table knife to cut a small section from a 2-inch plastic-foam ball. Use a plastic spice bottle for the body and glue the cut side of the head on top of the spice bottle cap.

2. Cut a small circle of fabric and glue it to the top of another bottle cap, forming a hat. Glue the hat to the top of the head. Add moveable plastic eyes and a fabric mouth.

3. Glue a piece of ribbon around the side of the spice bottle cap. Cut a piece of fabric for a dress to fit around the bottle. Put glue on the bottle below the ribbon and press the fabric into it.

4. To make the arms, cut two pieces from a chenille stick and insert them under the glued fabric of the dress. Add fabric gloves.

LACY BAG
(felt, lace, cording, beads)

1. From a large piece of felt, cut an 18-inch circle. Cut flower designs from a piece of lace and glue them near the center of the circle.

2. Using a paper punch, punch a hole about every other inch around the edge of the felt circle.

3. Lace one piece of cording in and out through the holes on one half of the circle, leaving the ends hanging loose. Lace another piece of cording through the other half.

4. At one half of the circle, thread a bead on two ends of cording and knot the ends together. Do the same for the other half.

5. Hold the cording ends in one hand. Push the fabric on the cording away from you with the other hand to form the bag.

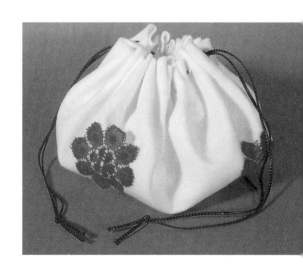

ROCK PAPERWEIGHT
(smooth rock, acrylic paint, fabric, fabric flower)

1. Wash and dry a smooth rock. Cover it with acrylic paint. Let dry.

2. Cut and glue a fabric strip around the rock, forming loops on top. Glue a small fabric flower in the center of the loops.

RAINBOW HEART HANGER
(paper, string)

1. Make a pattern by folding a sheet of paper in half and cutting out a heart. Then cut a heart out of the middle of the first heart, leaving a border heart.

2. Trace around the inside and outside of the border-heart pattern on black paper. Cut out the hearts, making several border hearts.

3. Trace around the outside of the heart border on white paper. Make half as many hearts as borders, and cut out the hearts. Color both sides of the hearts with markers.

4. Glue one colored heart in between two black border hearts along with a piece of string. Glue all the hearts together on a string.

VALENTINES FROM THE GARDEN
(construction paper, old seed catalog or magazine)

1. Fold a piece of construction paper in half. Fold it in half again the other way. Open the paper and lay it flat. Draw a heart in the lower right-hand square. Cut out the heart.

2. Fold the paper together so the heart opening is on the top layer and the fold is on the left.

3. Cut a flower picture from an old seed catalog or a magazine. Glue the picture behind the cutout heart. Write a message to go with your picture. For example, "My heart grows for you."

HEART NUT BOX
(half-gallon milk carton, construction paper, white glue and water, rickrack, tissue paper, nuts)

1. Measure 2 1/2 inches from the bottom of a half-gallon milk carton. Cut off the top of the carton and discard.

2. Tear red and pink construction paper into small pieces. Brush the pieces of paper with a mixture of white glue and a little water. Overlap the pieces on the box. Let dry.

3. Glue strips of rickrack and paper hearts around the box. Put tissue paper and nuts inside.

TISSUE FLOWERS
(tissue paper, chenille sticks, buttons)

1. To make the petals for each flower, cut eight circles of tissue paper, each about 4 inches in diameter. Poke a small hole through the middle of all the circles.

2. To make the stem and flower center, push a chenille stick through all the holes. Thread one end of the chenille stick up through one button hole and down through the other button hole, twisting the end around the stick just under the button.

3. Add a dab of glue at the flower center just under the button. Gather the tissues to create a conelike shape. Place a small piece of tape around the bottom of the cone and chenille stick stem.

HEART PIN GIFT AND CARD
(paper, felt, safety pin)

1. To make the card, fold a piece of white paper in half. Write a message and draw a border, leaving room for the heart pin in the center of the card.

2. Cut two matching hearts from red felt. Glue them together. The heart should fit on the front of the card.

3. Glue a safety pin in the middle of the heart. Glue a small strip of felt across the opened pin. Let dry.

4. Pin the heart to the front of the card.

SIGNED, "I LOVE YOU"
(paper, poster board)

Many people who have hearing difficulties use sign language to communicate. The sign language symbol for "I Love You" combines the letters *I, L,* and *Y* into one symbol.

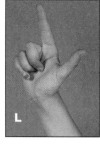

1. Trace around one of your hands on a piece of paper. Cut out the tracing.

2. From poster board, draw and cut out a heart large enough to fit the hand in the center. Glue the hand to the heart, leaving the ring and middle fingers unglued. Curl the two unglued fingers forward and glue the fingertips to the palm of the hand.

3. Cut another heart, larger than the first, from poster board and glue the first heart in the center. Write the message "I Love You!"

FLUTTERING HEART
(construction paper, crepe paper)

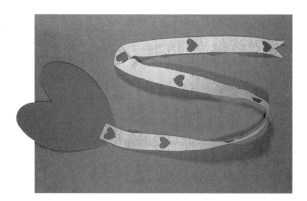

1. Draw and cut out a large heart from construction paper.

2. Cut a tail about one yard long from a roll of crepe paper. Staple the tail to the point of the heart.

3. Draw and cut out small hearts and glue them along the tail.

4. Go outdoors. Hold onto the tail and run. The heart will flutter in the wind.

VALENTINE BUTTERFLY MESSAGE
(construction paper, paper doily, poster paint, spring-type clothespin, chenille stick)

1. Cut a butterfly shape from red construction paper and decorate it with pieces from a paper doily.

2. Paint a spring-type clothespin red and let it dry. Glue the butterfly on one side of the clothespin. Add antennae made from a chenille stick.

3. Write a valentine greeting on a small, heart-shaped piece of paper, and glue it to the other side of the clothespin.

4. Clip the butterfly where it will surprise the person who is to receive it.

PET DISH

(plastic food container, fabric, rickrack)

1. Glue fabric from the top to the bottom on the outside of a plastic food container.

2. Cut out small fabric hearts from another piece of fabric and glue them around the sides of the container.

3. Add rickrack along the top and bottom as shown.

VALENTINE CANDY HOLDER

(plastic laundry detergent bottle, yarn, felt, candy)

1. *Ask an adult to help you* thoroughly clean a plastic laundry detergent bottle and to draw and cut out the shape shown in the diagram.

2. Use a paper punch to make holes around the edge of the plastic holder. Start at the center of the heart and loop yarn around the edge and through the holes, ending where you started. Tie the yarn ends into a bow.

3. Cut a strip of felt and glue it around the outside of the holder. Add a felt heart. Place wrapped candy inside the holder.

HEART HOTPAD

(paper, denim fabric, clear-drying glue, needle and embroidery floss, cotton)

1. Draw and cut out a large heart pattern from a piece of paper 8 inches square. Trace two of these hearts onto a piece of denim fabric.

2. Spread a clear-drying glue around the inside edge of each heart. Let dry, then carefully cut out each heart. (The glue will help keep the fabric from fraying.)

3. Start at the top of the heart. Sew the hearts together with an embroidery needle and six-strand embroidery floss, using a running stitch. Leave an opening.

4. Stuff some cotton between the two hearts, spreading the cotton evenly inside. Sew the opening shut.

5. Tie a bow at the top of the heart with the remaining floss.

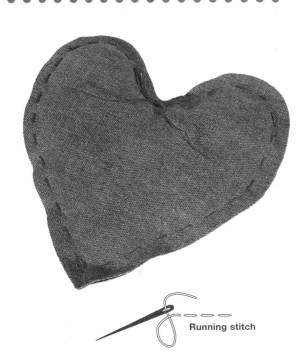

Running stitch

PAPER-DOLL VALENTINE
(construction paper)

1. Starting at the narrow end of a 5-by-12-inch piece of paper, fold over 1 1/2 inches of the paper. Continue to fold into accordion pleats until the whole piece is pleated.

2. Using a pencil, lightly sketch half of a doll shape. Be sure the center of the doll is on the fold and that the hands come out to the end of the paper.

3. Cut out the dolls with the paper folded. The dolls will be holding hands. On the front of each doll, glue a cutout paper letter, spelling *L O V E*.

VALENTINE NECKLACE
(white glue, aluminum foil, yarn)

1. Draw the shape of a heart with white glue on a piece of aluminum foil.

2. Press pieces of yarn into the glue-shaped heart, making a colorful design. Add a yarn loop. Brush the top of the yarn with glue and let dry completely.

3. Gently peel the heart away from the foil. Cut a long piece of yarn and thread it through the loop for the necklace. Tie the ends together.

VALENTINE MOUSE BOOKMARK
(construction paper, yarn)

1. Cut a rectangle from a piece of black construction paper. Fold one end of the rectangle.

2. Cut out and glue a red paper heart to the fold for a head. Add big ears, eyes, a nose, and whiskers to the head. Glue a piece of yarn to the other end of the rectangle for a tail.

3. Put the bookmark into a book, keeping the mouse's head above the top edge of the pages so it can "peek" at you.

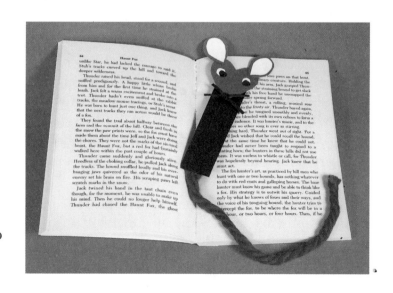

VALENTINE PORTRAIT
(poster board, construction paper, flashlight)

1. Fold a vertical strip of poster board into three equal sections. Cut two pieces of white construction paper to fit the middle section.

2. Put a lit flashlight on a table in a dark room. *Ask permission* to lightly tape one paper to a wall. Sit between the flashlight and the paper so your profile fits on the paper. Have a partner trace the outline of your silhouette on the paper.

3. Remove the paper from the wall and cut out the silhouette. Trace around the silhouette on a piece of black paper and cut it out. Glue the black silhouette to the second piece of white paper and then to the middle section of the poster board. Write your name and date below the silhouette.

4. Glue a heart at each corner. Make one more fold in the third section of poster board. Place the top of the first section in the fold and tape it so the portrait will stand up.

TREE OF SWEETHEARTS
(poster paint, poster board, construction paper)

1. Paint a tree trunk and limbs on a large piece of white poster board. Let dry.

2. Cut out hearts from construction paper. Write the name of a friend, a classmate, or a family member on each heart. Glue them to the tree.

3. Hang it on a bulletin board.

PIGGY-BANK VALENTINE CARD
(construction paper)

1. Draw and cut out a large circle for the pig's body and a small circle for the pig's head from construction paper. Glue them together.

2. Cut out ears, eyes, a nose, legs, and a tail from paper, and glue them to the pig's body. Draw on a mouth.

3. Decorate the pig by gluing on small red paper hearts. Draw a slot at the top of the pig.

4. Write this message on the back of the pig: "You can bank on me to be your Valentine!"

LACY RING VALENTINE
(construction paper, self-adhesive reinforcement rings)

1. To make the card, fold a piece of red construction paper in half. Draw and cut out a heart shape from pink paper and glue it onto the front of the card.

2. To make the lacy border, cut self-adhesive reinforcement rings in half. Remove the backing and place them around the pink heart.

3. Write a message inside the card.

HEART TOSS GAME
(February calendar page, construction paper, five candy hearts)

1. Glue a February calendar page on a piece of construction paper, or draw one yourself.

To play: Place the calendar in the center of a table. Standing a few feet away from the table, players take turns tossing five candy hearts onto the page. Add up the numbers in the boxes where the candies land. The player with the most points is the winner.

EGG CARTON JEWELRY BOX
(cardboard egg carton, fabric ruffle, lightweight cardboard, fabric, string of craft pearls)

1. Use a pink-colored cardboard egg carton for the jewelry box. Glue a 1 1/2-inch white fabric ruffle around the top edge of the lid.

2. Turn the box over and trace around the lid on a piece of lightweight cardboard. Cut out the cardboard. Cover one side of the cardboard with fabric, gluing the excess fabric on the underside.

3. Glue the covered cardboard on top of the jewelry box lid. Add a fabric-covered cardboard heart in the center.

4. Decorate the heart by gluing a string of craft pearls around the heart's edge.

THREE-SIDED HEART PICKS
(construction paper, round toothpicks, cake)

1. To make each heart pick, cut out three small hearts, one each from white, pink, and red construction paper.

2. Glue a round toothpick to the center of one heart. Fold the other two hearts in half. Glue one half of each heart to each side of the first heart at the back. Then glue the remaining two halves together.

3. Place the heart picks into a cake, making a design.

(Be sure to remove all the heart picks before cutting and serving the cake.)

VALENTINE RABBIT
(poster board, construction paper, cotton balls)

1. Fold a piece of white poster board in half to form a card.

2. Draw and cut out hearts of different sizes, shapes, and colors from construction paper to create a rabbit as shown.

3. Pull bits of cotton from cotton balls and glue to the ears, paws, legs, and tail of the rabbit.

4. Write a message inside such as, "I'm 'hopping' you will be my Valentine."

SWEETHEART PHOTO FRAME
(plastic-foam trays, paper, table knife, rickrack, construction paper, yarn)

1. Use a white plastic-foam tray for the base of the photo frame. Trim away the curved edges of a pink plastic-foam tray to fit inside the base.

2. Draw and cut out a heart shape from paper, making it small enough so that two hearts will fit on the pink section of the frame. Trace two hearts on the pink section, and carefully cut them out with a table knife. Tape a photo in each heart.

3. Glue the pink section to the base. Add rickrack and cut-paper hearts for decoration.

4. Poke two holes at the top of the frame and tie a piece of yarn through for a hanger.

HEART NOTEPAD
(poster board, paper, paper doily, ribbon)

1. To make the front and back cover of the notepad, fold a 7-by-14-inch piece of poster board in half. Draw a heart shape as shown in the photo and cut it out.

2. Trace the heart shape on a piece of white paper. Cut out the heart shape, trimming it slightly smaller so it will fit inside the notepad.

3. Cut out about twenty white paper hearts. Place them inside the notepad and staple them together at the top.

4. Decorate the cover of the notepad with pieces cut from a paper doily. Use a paper punch to punch a hole in the corner of the front cover. Tie on a piece of ribbon.

THREE-D VALENTINE CARD
(poster board, crayons)

1. Fold a piece of white poster board in half to make the card.

2. Cut out a heart shape from white poster board, color it with crayons, and write a message on it. Fold the heart in half with the message on the outside. Then fold the outside edges of the heart forward.

3. Glue the folded edges of the heart to the inside of the card, centering the fold of the heart on the fold of the card.

4. Open the card, and the heart will "pop out."

HEART CANDY BOX
(construction paper, small paper cup)

1. Cut two hearts from construction paper, making them slightly larger than the diameter of a small paper cup. Glue one heart to the bottom of the cup.

2. Draw and cut out a strip of paper for a hinge. Glue one end of the hinge to the side of the cup and one end to the second heart for a lid.

3. Lift the lid and place candies or other treats inside.

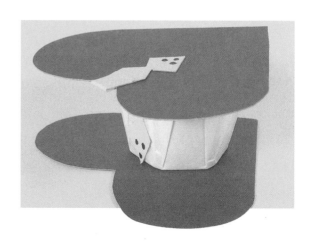

POTATO PRINT STATIONERY
(potato, table knife, poster paint, envelope and writing paper)

1. Cut a clean potato in half. With a pencil, draw a different-sized heart on each half.

2. *Ask an adult to help you* use a table knife to cut away the area around the hearts, leaving them about 1/2 inch higher than the rest of the potato.

3. Cover the hearts with poster paint, and press them onto a piece of writing paper or an envelope. Repeat until you have the design you want. Let dry.

FABRIC FLOWERS
(thin wire, small bottle, paper plate, lightweight fabric, chenille sticks, white tape, permanent marker)

1. To make each petal, wrap a 3-inch thin, flexible wire around a small bottle that is about 1 1/2 inches in diameter. Twist the ends of the wire together and slide it off the bottle. Bend the ends upward so the wire looks like an egg holder. Repeat this process six times.

2. Squeeze some white glue on a paper plate. Hold the wire ends and dip the petal in the glue. Place each petal on a piece of lightweight red fabric with the wire ends up and let dry.

3. To make the stamens, cut 2-inch pieces from a white chenille stick and bend them in half. For the stem, use a long green chenille stick. Wrap one end of the stem around the stamens and twist to hold.

4. With scissors trim the fabric around the outer edge of each petal. Straighten the wire ends. Cut two leaves with long stems from green felt.

5. Use a permanent marker to color the white tape green. Place three petals and one leaf on each side of the flower stem. Wrap the wire ends and leaves with the tape. Bend the stem in a spiral shape until the flower will stand.

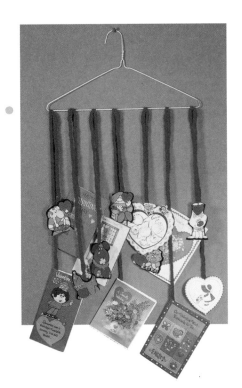

A VALENTINE MOBILE
(wire clothes hanger, yarn, Valentine cards)

1. Cut a long piece of yarn for every two Valentine cards you have received.

2. Tie the pieces of yarn onto the crossbar of the hanger, leaving all the ends hanging at different lengths.

3. Tape one card to each end of yarn. Spread the tied yarn sections out evenly across the crossbar.

SWEETHEART HOUSE
(construction paper, large facial tissue box, paper, fabric ruffle, bead,
half-gallon milk carton, toothpaste box, cotton ball)

1. To make the base of the house, glue white construction paper around the outside of a large, rectangular facial tissue box. Decorate the box with paper and markers. Glue pieces of ruffle at the windows for curtains. Glue a bead to the door for a doorknob.

2. For the roof, measure 5 inches from the bottom of a half-gallon milk carton. Cut off the top and discard. Draw a line diagonally across the bottom of the carton. Cut on the line and up each side seam, making two triangular sections. Place the sections together, overlapping a little to fit the length of the top of the house. Glue the sections together where they overlap and let dry. Cover the roof with paper and draw shingles with a marker. Glue the roof to the top of the house and let dry.

3. To make the chimney, glue paper around a toothpaste box and decorate with paper and markers. Use some cotton from a cotton ball for smoke. Glue the chimney to the side of the house.

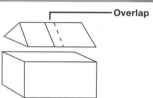

Overlap

PENCIL VALENTINE
(paper, pinking shears, poster paint, pencil)

1. Draw and cut out two identical paper hearts. Use pinking shears for a saw-toothed edge.

2. Paint "Be Mine" in the center of one heart.

3. Glue the two hearts together with the pencil in between. Let dry.

VALENTINE CROWN
(construction paper)

1. Cut out and tape together a 2-inch-wide strip of red construction paper to fit around your head.

2. Cut two strips of paper, each 1 inch by 12 inches. Fold one strip in half and make a 2-inch slit in the center. Glue the strip from one side of the headband to the other.

3. Glue the second strip so the headband is divided into quarters. Tuck and glue the center of the second strip into the slit of the first. Cut out a paper heart and glue it in the center where the two strips cross.

4. Add white cut-paper hearts to the crown.

CHENILLE-STICK DOLL
(three chenille sticks, construction paper, yarn, buttons, moveable plastic eyes)

1. To make the body and legs of the doll, place two long chenille sticks next to each other and twist them together from one end about three quarters of the length of the sticks. Spread the two untwisted ends apart for legs.

2. To make arms, wrap one chenille stick around the middle of the body.

3. Cut two identical hearts from construction paper for the body. Then cut sets of two smaller hearts for the head, shoes, and hands. Glue the hearts together with the chenille sticks in between them. Glue a piece of yarn between the hearts at the top of the head.

4. Add details with buttons, markers, cutout paper hearts, and moveable plastic eyes.

VALENTINE DESIGN
(poster board, tissue paper, white glue and water)

1. Cut a rectangular piece of white poster board.

2. Cut several hearts the same size from various colors of tissue paper.

3. Make a mixture of half white glue and half water. Brush the mixture on each heart and arrange them on the poster board.

VALENTINE GARLAND
(construction paper, pinking shears, string)

1. Cut out pairs of different-colored construction paper hearts of various sizes, using scissors to make straight or scalloped edges and pinking shears for a saw-toothed edge.

2. Glue the heart pairs together with a long piece of string between them. Let dry.

3. Hang the valentine garland over a doorway or a window.

HEART COASTERS
(clear plastic lids, heavy white paper, old flower catalog)

1. For each coaster, trace around a clear plastic lid on heavy white paper. Cut out the circle and trim so it fits snugly inside the lid. Remove the paper circle.

2. Find a flower picture in an old flower catalog. Trace the paper circle around the picture. Cut out the flower circle and then cut it into a heart shape. Glue the heart on top of the paper circle.

3. Press the paper circle, with the flower facing up, inside the clear plastic lid.

GLITTERING HEART PIN
(poster board, glitter, safety pin)

1. Draw and cut out a heart shape from a piece of poster board.

2. Spread one side of the heart with glue and sprinkle it with glitter. Let it dry and then shake off any loose glitter.

3. Tape a safety pin to the back of the heart.

A BIG VALENTINE HUG
(paper plate, yarn, paper doily, construction paper)

1. Draw a face on a paper plate and glue cut pieces of yarn around the plate rim for hair. Cut a paper doily in half and glue it to the bottom of the back of the paper plate for a collar.

2. Tape pieces of construction paper together, making a long strip for arms. Glue the head in the middle of the arms. Draw and cut out paper hands and glue them to the ends of the arms.

3. Cut two small paper doilies in half and glue them to both arms for cuffs.

4. Write a valentine message below the collar so that the arms, when folded, will cover your message.

A Great Big Valentine Hug! Love, Sue

VALENTINE RECIPE CARDS
(index cards, permanent markers)

1. Decorate index cards by drawing a border of hearts along the edges using different-colored permanent markers.

2. Make a set of cards, writing your favorite "sweet" recipes to give to a relative or a friend.

DOORKNOB DECORATION
(fabric, pinking shears, cotton balls, yarn)

1. Cut four identical hearts from colorful fabric. Use pinking shears for a saw-toothed edge.

2. Glue cotton balls in the center of two of the hearts. Squeeze some glue around the edges of the hearts.

3. Cut a piece of yarn and place one end in the center of each heart. Put the remaining two fabric hearts on top of the yarn and cotton balls. Press the edges together and let dry.

4. Use the yarn to hang the hearts on a doorknob.

PLASTIC BIRDHOUSE
(2-liter plastic beverage bottle with black base, felt)

1. *Ask an adult to help you* cut the top off a 2-liter plastic beverage bottle.

2. Look at the base of the bottle. There should be three small holes in the base. If there aren't any, *ask an adult to help* poke a hole in the base.

3. Cut hearts and rectangles from pieces of felt. Glue them to the outside of the bottle.

4. *Ask an adult to help you* hang the birdhouse outside by mounting the base on a nail under a roof eve as shown.

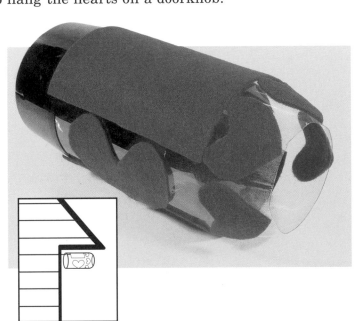

HEART-IN-HAND VALENTINES
(construction paper, buttons, lace, fabric)

1. With a pencil, trace around your hand and wrist on construction paper. Repeat for as many valentines as you wish to make. Cut along each hand outline. Draw and cut out a heart and glue it onto the palm of each hand.

2. Draw and cut out rectangular pieces of paper and glue them on each wrist for a cuff. Add buttons and pieces of lace and fabric.

3. Write a message on the back of each paper hand and give it to someone special.

HEART-SHAPED PINECONE WREATH
(cardboard, waxed paper, paper plate, pinecones, ribbon, heavy white paper, plastic-foam tray, large needle)

1. Draw and cut out a heart shape from cardboard to make the base of the wreath as shown in the diagram.

2. Cover your work space with waxed paper. Squeeze glue onto a paper plate. Using pinecones that have flat tops, dip each top in the glue and place it on the wreath base until the base is covered. Let dry for at least one day.

3. Tape ribbon to the back of the wreath and wrap it around the pinecones. Make a bow and tie it to the wreath. Glue a loop of ribbon to the back for a hanger.

4. Cut hearts from heavy white paper. Place each heart on a plastic-foam tray. Using a large needle, punch a design on the hearts. Glue them to the wreath.

SECRET HEARTS VALENTINE
(construction paper, old flower catalog)

1. Fold a large sheet of construction paper in half. Keeping the paper folded, cut out half of a heart. Open to find a large heart.

2. Refold the heart and glue pictures cut from an old flower catalog around the edge of the half heart. In the center write "Roses are red...violets are blue..."

3. Cut out a small heart pattern. Open the large heart. Trace around the small pattern five times on the right half of the inside of the card. Cut out the hearts.

4. Fold the card and turn it over. Trace through the five cutout hearts to make five hearts on the left inside the large folded heart. Open the card. Write one word inside each heart: "Hey, Valentine, I like you."

5. Trace around the small heart pattern, making several more hearts around your valentine message. Write a word inside each heart.

6. Open the card. Draw a dotted line down the center fold. Write "Fold here to read a secret message for you."

CUPID POP-UP
(plastic-foam cup, tongue depressor, construction paper, paper bag, gift wrap)

1. In the bottom of a plastic-foam cup, cut a slit just big enough to fit a tongue depressor through.

2. To make Cupid, draw and cut out construction paper wings that will fit inside the cup. Cut out a head, arms, and body half in one piece from a paper bag. Glue the shape on the wings. Add features with markers and paper. Glue Cupid to the tongue depressor.

3. Decorate the outside of the cup with pieces of gold gift wrap and paper.

BOOK OF HEARTS
(cardboard, fabric, construction paper, ribbon, felt)

1. Cut two pieces of cardboard slightly larger than a sheet of construction paper for the front and back cover of the book.

2. Glue fabric to one side of each cardboard, wrapping and gluing the excess fabric around to the back. Let dry.

3. With a paper punch, punch two holes in each cover. Punch holes in several sheets of construction paper, making sure all the holes line up.

4. Place the paper between the covers. Thread a piece of ribbon through the holes and tie a bow. Cut out heart-shaped pieces of felt and glue them to the front cover.

5. Glue or tape the valentines you receive inside the book.

VALENTINE RINGTOSS
(paper towel tube, poster paint, ribbon, plastic scoop, construction paper, heavy paper plate, three plastic lids)

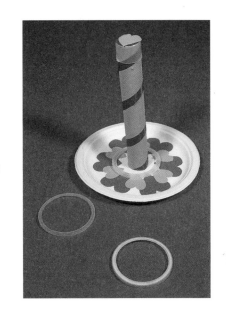

1. Cover a paper towel tube with pink poster paint and let dry. Glue a piece of red ribbon around the tube as shown. Cut the handle off a clear plastic scoop from a dry beverage-drink mix, and push the scoop over one end of the tube. Add a construction paper heart to the top.

2. Glue the open tube end to the center of a heavy paper plate and let dry. Decorate the plate with hearts cut from pink and red paper.

3. Cut the centers out of the three plastic lids, leaving the rims, to make rings.

To play: Place the plate a few feet from you on the floor. Have each player take a turn tossing three rings onto the tube. Make the game more challenging by moving farther from the plate.

Special Valentines

Create unique keepsake valentines for those people who are special to you.

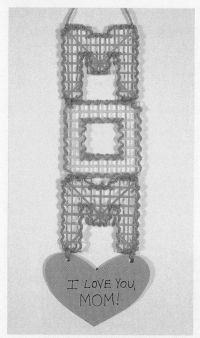

JUST FOR MOM
(three plastic berry baskets, yarn, large-eyed needle, paper)

1. Cut the bottom sections from three plastic berry baskets that have a square design. Cut out areas from the basket to form the block letters *M O M* as shown.

2. Thread a piece of yarn on a large-eyed sewing needle. Weave the yarn around the edges of each letter, tying the ends together when finished.

3. Tie each letter one above the other with yarn. Add a piece of yarn to the top of the first letter *M* for a hanger.

4. Draw and cut out a paper heart. Write "I love you, Mom!" on it. Punch two holes in the heart and tie it to the bottom of the second letter *M*.

LOLLIPOPS FOR SISTER
(five lollipops, tongue depressor, fabric, yarn, paper, felt, chenille stick)

1. Glue five lollipops to a tongue depressor, making legs, arms, and a head. Let dry overnight.

2. Cut pieces of fabric and wrap around the tongue depressor and lollipop body. Glue in place. Add a yarn belt.

3. Add paper eyes and a felt mouth. Glue pieces of a chenille stick to the top of the head for hair.

4. From fabric and paper, make a square sign that says "Sister, you're sweet!" Glue the sign to a piece of chenille stick and glue the stick to a lollipop arm.

CITYSCAPE FOR DAD
(poster board, plastic-foam tray, acrylic paint)

1. Cut a rectangle about 6 inches by 13 1/2 inches from poster board. Fold in half to measure 6 inches by 7 inches.

2. Draw and cut out a city skyline from a black plastic-foam tray. Glue it to the front of the card. Add "lit" windows with acrylic paint and let dry. Cut and glue a crescent moon in place.

3. Inside the card, write "Dad, you're one in a million! Happy Valentine's Day!" and add your signature.

A BAT FOR BROTHER
(poster board, masking tape)

1. Draw and cut out a baseball bat shape about 17 inches long from a piece of orange poster board. Wrap masking tape around the handle area. Fold the baseball bat into three equal sections.

2. Cut out a circle from white poster board and draw on baseball stitching with a marker. On the ball write "Brother, you're an MVP." Glue it on the end of the bat as shown.

3. Open the sections of the bat, and write inside "My Valentine Pal!" and add your signature.

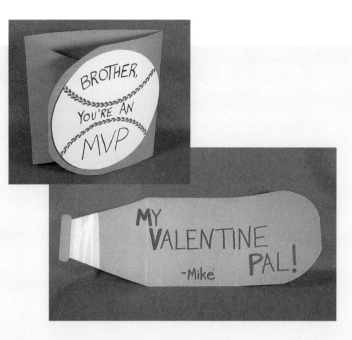

SUN CATCHER FOR GRANDMA
(1-liter plastic bottle, tissue paper, yarn, paper)

1. Cut off the bottom curved section of a 1-liter plastic bottle and discard. Carefully cut shapes from colorful tissue paper. Brush a little glue on them and arrange them on the bottle.

2. Tie two pieces of yarn at the neck of the bottle opposite each other for a hanger. Knot the ends together.

3. Using a paper punch, punch two holes opposite each other near the bottom edge. Cut a heart from paper and write "Grandma, be my Valentine!" Punch two holes in the top of the heart. Tie the heart with yarn to the two holes at the bottom of the bottle.

MEET THE BEST GRANDPA
(poster board, old magazines, aluminum foil)

1. Cut a 10-by-20-inch rectangle from poster board and fold it in half to make a 10-inch square card.

2. Decorate the front of the card with magazine cutouts of grandpa-like pictures from around the world. Add two paper hearts. Write "OPEN to meet the best grandpa in the WORLD!"

3. Open the card. On the left side, cut and glue a heart with the message "Happy Valentine's Day!" On the right side, cut and glue a large aluminum-foil heart in the center. Add a small paper heart in each corner.

4. Write the word "You!" above the foil heart. Sign your name under the heart.

Valentines You Can Wear

It's always fun to dress up on a special day. Create these festive clothes and accessories for yourself. Or make someone a gift to wear.

HAT AND GLOVE SET
(plastic-foam trays, toothpick, yarn, large-eyed needle, knitted hat and gloves)

1. Draw and cut out several hearts from clean white plastic-foam trays. Poke a hole in the top of each heart with a toothpick.

2. Thread a long piece of yarn through the needle.

3. Loosely attach each heart by threading the yarn through the hole, then through the knitted fabric. Tie a knot in the yarn and cut the ends.

4. Attach four hearts to the top of the hat and one to the side of each glove.

SWEETHEART SOCKS
(felt, socks, fabric glue)

1. Using three different colors of felt, cut three different-sized heart shapes.

2. Lay the socks flat with the cuffs folded down.

3. Glue the larger heart first to each cuff. Then add the others. Let dry.

VALENTINE FOOTWEAR
(paper, cloth sneakers, permanent or fabric markers)

1. Draw heart designs on a piece of paper and cut them out.

2. With a pencil, lightly trace the hearts on a pair of sneakers.

3. Trace around the hearts with markers. Don't press too hard, or the marker may spread over the cloth.

FLOWERED GARDEN GLOVES

(flowered fabric, fabric glue, cloth gloves, yarn,
needle and thread, permanent marker)

1. Cut out flowers from fabric. Use fabric glue to attach a flower to the end of each finger on a pair of cloth gloves. Add more flowers near the cuffs.

2. Cut two small pieces of yarn. Tie them loosely around the ring finger of each glove, making a bow. With a needle and thread, sew around the bow to hold it in place.

3. Wrap some yarn around four of your fingers. Pull the yarn off and sew around the center to make a bow. Attach a bow at each cuff.

4. Draw bugs on the gloves with permanent marker.

HEART PRINT SHIRT

(cardboard, cotton shirt, cellulose sponge, fabric paint, paper plate)

1. Place a large piece of cardboard inside a cotton shirt, stretching it tight.

2. Using scissors, cut a heart shape from a hard cellulose sponge.

3. Squeeze a small amount of fabric paint on a paper plate. Dip the sponge heart in the paint. Then press the heart on the front of the shirt, making a design. Let dry.

4. Repeat the process and add hearts to the sleeves or neck of the shirt.

BOLO TIE

(large button with shank, aluminum foil, construction paper, shoestring)

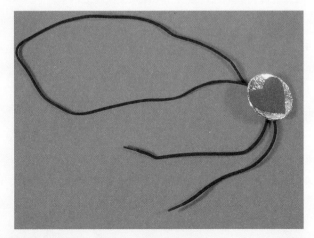

1. Cover a large button with aluminum foil, leaving the shank exposed.

2. Cut a heart from construction paper. Glue it on the button.

3. Fold a long shoestring in half. Thread the ends through the shank of the button.

4. Push the button up the shoestring near the neck of your shirt.

Table Decorations

Decorate the table for Valentine's Day with some heart-shaped accessories.

TABLETOP VALENTINES

(construction paper, glitter, paper doily, plastic straws, chenille sticks, felt, laundry detergent cap, ribbon, clay)

1. Cut hearts of different sizes from construction paper. Decorate them with other colors of paper, glitter, or a section from a paper doily. Glue them to plastic straws.

2. Twist a white and a red chenille stick together, then shape them into a heart. You can also make a heart from just one chenille stick. Glue the chenille-stick ends into one end of a plastic straw. Let dry.

3. Glue felt around the outside of a clean laundry detergent cap. Add ribbon. Fill the cap with clay. Push the straws into the clay.

FABRIC-HEART PLACE MAT

(paper, fabric, fabric ruffle)

1. Draw and cut out a large paper heart pattern about the size of a place mat and a smaller heart large enough to cover the handles of a fork, a knife, and a spoon.

2. Pin the heart patterns on fabric. Carefully trace around the hearts with fabric glue, being sure not to get glue on the paper. Remove the paper patterns. Let the glue dry overnight.

3. Cut around the fabric hearts close to the line of dried glue. (The glue will prevent the fabric edges from fraying.) Glue a fabric ruffle around the edge of the large fabric heart.

4. Glue the smaller heart on the left side of the large heart, leaving an opening at the top for the utensils.

PERSONALIZED TABLECLOTH

(paper tablecloth, poster board, old newspapers, permanent markers)

1. Cut a large paper tablecloth to fit your table.

2. Draw and cut out a place mat-sized heart pattern from poster board.

3. Place the tablecloth on old newspapers. Using permanent markers, trace around the heart pattern once for each place setting.

4. Add a name and features to each of the place settings, one for each guest.

FELT-HEART CENTERPIECE
(felt)

1. Cut six identical hearts from white, red, and pink felt.

2. Lay the hearts in a circle with the edges of the hearts overlapping slightly.

3. Glue the hearts together at the overlapped areas. Let dry.

SALT AND PEPPER SHAKERS
(cardboard salt and pepper shakers, paper)

1. Cover the outsides of cardboard salt and pepper shakers with white paper.

2. Cut out various-sized paper hearts and glue them to one side of each shaker, making a valentine character. Add a small heart to the top of each shaker, leaving the hole area open.

3. On the opposite side of the pepper shaker, glue a paper heart with the message "I'll pepper you with love!" On the salt shaker, glue a paper heart with the message "You're worth your salt to me!"

HEART NAPKIN HOLDER
(one-quart milk carton, construction paper)

1. Draw a pencil line 1 1/2 inches from the bottom around a one-quart milk carton.

2. Cut out a paper heart pattern. Place the point of the heart on one side of the carton, 1 inch up from the bottom, and trace around the heart. Do this again on the opposite side. Cut out as shown.

3. Cut out a 1-inch section or slot from the two carton sides without hearts.

4. Lay the carton on paper and trace around the heart and base of the carton. Cut out the tracing and glue it to the carton. Add more paper hearts.

5. Place dinner napkins in the slots.

DOILY BASKET
(construction paper, paper doily)

1. On a sheet of construction paper, trace around a plate that is slightly smaller than the diameter of a paper doily. Cut out the circle.

2. Glue the paper circle in the center of the doily and let dry. Fold the circle in half with the doily on the outside.

3. Divide the fold line into thirds as shown in Diagram 1. Fold up a corner of the doily as shown in Diagram 2. Then fold each corner to the back of the doily along the same crease lines. Tuck the corners of the doily to the inside along the crease lines as shown in Diagram 3.

4. Staple a strip of paper to the inside of the basket for a handle.

Diagram 1

Diagram 2

Diagram 3

BUTTERFLY HEARTS
(poster board, construction paper, chenille stick, moveable plastic eyes)

1. Cut and fold a piece of poster board in half for a card.

2. Draw and cut out a butterfly's body from black construction paper. Glue it to the center of the front of the card. Add a small paper heart for a head.

3. Cut two pieces from a chenille stick for the antennae and glue them in place. Add two moveable plastic eyes.

4. Draw and cut out five paper hearts of various sizes and colors for each wing. Glue one heart on top of another, and then glue a wing to each side of the butterfly's body.

5. Write a message on the front of and inside the card.

VALENTINE'S DAY BANNER
(felt, fabric glue, wooden dowel, cording)

1. Cut three identical pieces of felt. Place them in a vertical position, overlapping the edges about 1 inch. Glue them together with fabric glue.

2. Fold the top edge of the first piece of felt over a wooden dowel. Glue in place and let dry.

3. Cut and glue felt flowers, stems, and leaves to the first section, a felt candy box to the second section, and a felt heart to the third section. Add pieces of yarn glued in place to spell "Be Mine."

4. Tie a piece of cording around each end of a wooden dowel for a hanger.

CUPID'S ARROW GAME
(round cardboard container, construction paper, poster board, wooden clothespins)

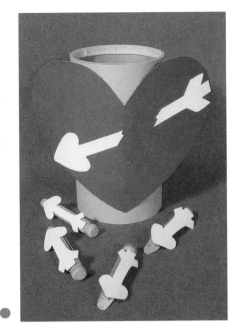

1. Cover a round cardboard container with pink construction paper.

2. Cut out a red heart from poster board and glue it to one side of the container. Draw and cut out a white arrow. Glue it on the heart as shown in the photo.

3. Draw and cut out four white arrows from poster board. Glue each one on a wooden clothespin with the point of the arrow at the opening of the clothespin.

To play: Stand with the container on the floor in front of you. Hold an arrow at chest height and drop it, trying to get it in the container. See who can get all of Cupid's arrows in the container.

YARN VALENTINE
(heavy white paper, yarn)

1. Fold a piece of heavy white paper to make a long vertical card. Scallop the edges with scissors.

2. With glue, draw a large heart with a smaller heart inside. Press a piece of yarn in the glue of each heart shape. Squeeze glue in the area between the two yarn hearts. Add small pieces of cut yarn.

3. Cut a long piece of yarn. Tie it into a bow and glue it to the top of the card and over the yarn-filled heart.

4. Write a message inside.

RED BIRD
(plastic cup, string, cellulose sponge, feathers, permanent marker, paper)

1. Use a ballpoint pen to make two small holes in the bottom of a plastic cup. Cut a 2-foot piece of string. Push one string end in each hole, tie a knot at one end, and let the string hang down inside the cup. Cut a 1-inch square of cellulose sponge. Tie it to the other end of the string.

2. Glue on a feather, covering the holes and string. Glue feathers to the sides of the cup for wings. Draw eyes with a permanent black marker. Cut a beak from black paper and glue in place.

3. To make the bird chirp, wet the sponge. Hold the cup in one hand. With your other hand, fold the sponge around the string. Slowly move the sponge down the string with a jerking movement to make the chirping noise.

VALENTINE BOOKMARK CARD
(construction paper)

1. To make the card, fold a piece of red construction paper in half. Cut a 3-inch slit in the middle of the front of the card.

2. Write on the card "Use my heart to mark your place." Write your name on the inside.

3. To make the bookmark, fold a 3-inch square of pink paper in half. Draw the outline of half a heart. Draw another smaller heart inside the first heart. Cut on both lines. Decorate the heart and slip it into the slit in the card.

VALENTINE SEQUIN PIN
(cardboard, tissue paper, sequins, ribbon, safety pin)

1. Cut a small heart shape from cardboard. Glue red tissue paper on both sides. Add sequins and let dry.

2. Cut a piece of ribbon, fold it in half, and glue the ends to the back of the heart. Tie a ribbon bow and glue it to the ribbon loop.

3. Attach a safety pin to the back of the ribbon loop.

YARN VASE
(plastic detergent bottle, yarn, felt)

1. *Ask an adult to help you* cut off the top of a small, clean plastic detergent bottle.

2. Start at the bottom of the bottle and spread a little glue around the outside. Press the end of a long piece of yarn into the glue. Continue until the bottle is covered.

3. Cut out a stem and leaves from pieces of yarn. Glue them to the vase. Add pieces of felt for a flower. Let dry overnight.

HEART ICE-CREAM-STICK HOLDER
(round cardboard container, ice-cream sticks, ribbon, felt, paper doily)

1. Cover the outside of a round cardboard container with glue and ice-cream sticks. Let dry.

2. Cut and glue a piece of ribbon at the top and bottom of the container. Cut hearts from felt and glue in place. Glue small hearts cut from sections of a paper doily on top of the felt hearts.

3. Fill the container with pencils, pens, markers, and other items.

FABRIC PHOTO FRAME
(cardboard, fabric, cotton balls, fabric ruffle)

1. Cut two 5-by-7-inch pieces of cardboard. Draw and cut out a heart shape from one cardboard so that a 3 1/2-by-5-inch photo will fill the shape.

2. To make the front of the frame, pull cotton balls apart and glue them around the cutout heart. Cover the cotton with fabric, gluing the fabric to the back of the cardboard. Carefully cut out the fabric from the center of the heart as shown. Glue the fabric tabs to the back of the cardboard.

3. To make the back of the frame, glue fabric to one side of the other piece of cardboard. Glue fabric ruffle around the edges and let dry.

4. Put the front and back of the frame together with the fabric facing out. Glue the sides and bottoms together, leaving the top of the frame open.

5. Cover a small piece of cardboard with fabric and glue it to the back for the stand. Slide a photo in the top of the frame to fill the cutout heart.

VALENTINE MOBILE
(construction paper, string)

1. Fold a sheet of construction paper in half, then in half again.

2. Following the diagram, draw the design along the two folded edges (the dotted lines) as shown. Cut along the solid lines only.

3. Unfold and pick up the outside strips at A and B, letting the rest drop down. Insert a piece of string for a hanger. Push out and press down the heart-shaped cutouts.

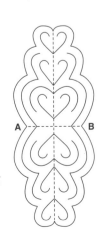

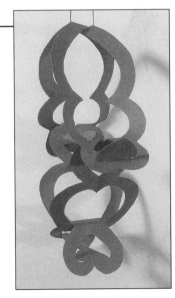

PUNCHED-CARD VALENTINES
(paper)

1. Fold a piece of paper in half to make a card. Keeping the card folded, punch holes with a paper punch all around the edges, leaving an unpunched section in the center.

2. Draw a picture or write a valentine message on the front. Open the card and write your name inside.

NECKLACE OF HEARTS
(string, construction paper)

1. Cut a piece of white string long enough to slip over your head with the ends tied together.

2. From red construction paper, cut pairs of identical hearts.

3. Glue one heart to the string. Glue the other heart on top of the first with the string in between. Continue until the string is covered with hearts.

VALENTINE KITE
(brown paper bag, old newspaper, poster paint,
self-adhesive reinforcement rings, two chenille sticks, cording, wooden dowel)

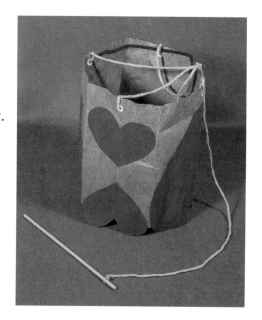

1. Draw a pencil line around a brown paper bag about 4 inches up from the bottom. Cut off the bottom section, and then cut a 1-inch strip from it. Glue the strip on the outside edge of the bag.

2. At the other end of the paper bag, draw a large heart on each large panel and a small heart on each side panel with the tops of the hearts on the bottom of the paper bag. Trim around the hearts as shown by the dotted line in the diagram.

3. Draw a small heart at the other end of the side panel, between the 1-inch strip and the other small heart. Paint the hearts with red poster paint. Let dry.

4. Punch a hole in the center of each panel through the 1-inch strip of paper. Place a self-adhesive reinforcement ring on both sides of each hole.

5. Staple a chenille stick inside the bag along each side panel on the 1-inch strip.

6. Cut four pieces of cording and tie one end of each piece through each of the four holes. Gather the other ends together and tie one long piece of cording around them. Tie the other end of the long piece of cording to one end of a wooden dowel.

7. Go outside. Holding the end of the wooden dowel, run or stand in the wind and watch your valentine kite flutter in the breeze.

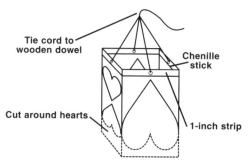

Tie cord to wooden dowel

Chenille stick

Cut around hearts

1-inch strip

BUTTON CARD
(poster board, construction paper, buttons)

1. Cut a piece of poster board slightly larger than a sheet of construction paper. Glue the paper in the center of the poster board. Fold in half, forming a card.

2. Cut the right edge of the card with scissors, making a scalloped design.

3. On the front of the card, arrange buttons of various sizes and colors in a heart shape. Glue them to the card.

4. Write a message inside.

PUFFY HEART MAGNET
(plastic lid, paper doily, cardboard, cotton balls, fabric, magnetic strip)

1. Cut out a heart shape from the center of a plastic lid. Trace around the plastic heart on a paper doily and cut out the heart. Glue the paper-doily heart on top of the plastic heart.

2. Draw and cut out a cardboard heart smaller than the plastic-lid heart. Glue cotton balls on one side. Cover the cotton balls with a heart-shaped piece of fabric, gluing it to the back of the cardboard.

3. Glue the fabric heart in the center of the plastic heart. Glue a magnetic strip to the back of the plastic heart.

CANDLE HOLDER
(tissue paper, white glue and water, glass bottle, nail polish, candle, sand)

1. Cut hearts from different-colored tissue paper. Brush a mixture of white glue and water on each piece. Press the pieces around the sides of a small glass bottle, overlapping some. Let them dry.

2. Paint the rim of the bottle with nail polish and let dry.

3. Stand a candle in the bottom of the bottle and pour sand around it to hold it in place.

DOORKNOB SURPRISE
(construction paper, yarn)

1. Cut a sheet of construction paper in half. Fold over 1 inch at the top. Using scissors, cut 1-inch slits at the bottom of the paper.

2. Cut a piece of white yarn about 1 1/2 feet long. Place the yarn in the fold at the top and glue in place. Tie the ends in a bow for a hanger.

3. Write a message with glue and press yarn into the glue. Add paper hearts. When dry, hang on a doorknob.

HEART SNACK HOLDERS
(plastic lids, permanent markers, spring-type clothespins)

1. Cut heart shapes from the centers of plastic lids. Decorate them with permanent markers. Write the name of the food or snack in the center of each lid.

2. Glue each plastic heart on a spring-type clothespin and let dry.

3. Place snacks in small bags and clip a heart holder to the top of each one to keep the bags sealed.

THREE-D FRAMED FLOWERS
(cardboard, picture frame, fabric, felt, button, fabric netting, chenille sticks, balloons, plastic cap, cardboard egg carton, candy, plastic berry basket, yarn, construction paper)

1. Cover a piece of cardboard from a picture frame with fabric. Place the cardboard in the frame. Cut a vase shape from felt and glue it in place, leaving the top open. Add fabric trim, making a flower with a button for the center.

2. Glue on a piece of fabric netting for the background. Cut and glue green felt leaves to green chenille sticks for flower stems.

3. Make one flower by gluing four balloons together with a plastic cap in the center. Create another flower using one cup section from a cardboard egg carton. Glue candy in the center.

4. Make a round-shaped flower by cutting a circle from the bottom of a plastic berry basket. Weave a piece of yarn in and out of the sections. Create another flower from construction paper.

HOLIDAY TISSUE BOX
(construction paper, 4 1/2-inch square tissue box, lace)

1. Cut and glue pink construction paper around all sides of a 4 1/2-inch-square vertical tissue box. Carefully trim around the tissue opening.

2. Draw and cut out two identical paper hearts for each side of the box. Glue one heart on top of the other in the center. Slightly curl up the edges of the top heart.

3. Cut small flowers from a piece of lace and glue one in the center of each heart. Add small paper hearts around the tissue opening.

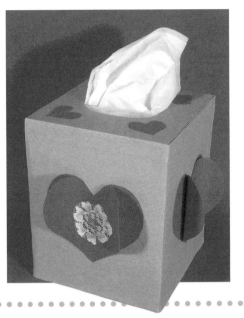

NEEDLE-PUNCHED CARD
(construction paper, tracing paper, plastic-foam tray, large needle)

1. Cut a heart shape from a folded sheet of red construction paper so that the top of the heart is on the fold.

2. Lay tracing paper on the heart and print a message, such as "Be My Valentine?" Add a design around the edges. Turn the tracing paper over so the message is backward.

3. Place the double heart and tracing paper on a piece of plastic-foam tray. With a large needle, poke holes along the pencil lines through the tracing paper and both hearts.

4. Remove the tracing paper and turn the card over. The card will have an interesting raised-dot effect on the front.

HAIR CLIP
(2 1/2-inch metal barrette base, plastic lid, felt, fabric, ribbon, rubber bands)

1. Remove the old ribbon from a metal barrette base.

2. Draw and cut out a heart shape from a plastic lid. Cut a smaller heart from felt and glue it on top of the plastic. Cut a smaller heart from fabric and glue it on top of the felt.

3. Cut a piece of ribbon. Tie it into a bow and glue it on top of the fabric heart.

4. Glue the heart to the metal barrette base and hold in place with rubber bands until dry.

CATERPILLAR VALENTINE
(construction paper)

1. Draw and cut out a leaf shape from construction paper. Draw and cut out four small red paper hearts and one pink paper heart.

2. Glue the four red hearts right side up and slightly overlapping along the leaf to form the caterpillar's body. Glue the pink heart upside down at one end of the red hearts for the head.

3. Cut eyes and a mouth from paper and glue them on the head.

4. Write "Valentine . . . Don't ever 'leaf' me!" and add your signature.

POTTED PACKET
(plastic flowerpot and base, construction paper, potting soil, flower seed packet, tongue depressor)

1. Decorate the sides of a plastic flowerpot with cutout hearts from different-colored construction paper.

2. Fill the flowerpot with potting soil.

3. Tape a flower seed packet to a wooden tongue depressor. Decorate the seed packet with cutout paper hearts.

4. Press the end of the tongue depressor into the potting soil.

HEART BELL
(plastic-foam tray, string, bells)

1. Draw and cut out a large heart from a pink plastic-foam tray. Draw a smaller heart inside the larger one and carefully cut it out.

2. Punch a hole in the top center of the large heart and tie a string for a hanger.

3. Punch other holes along the inside top edge of the heart. Tie a string to a bell and then attach the other end of the string to a hole. Tie the bells at different lengths.

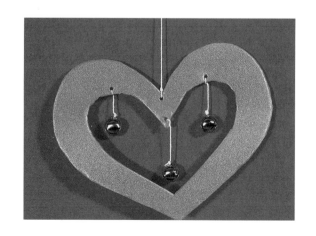

FABRIC JEWELRY BOX
(lightweight fabric, candy box with cardboard lid,
pinking shears, rickrack, lace)

1. Cut a piece of lightweight fabric big enough to cover the sides and top of a cardboard candy-box lid. Squeeze glue around the sides of the box and press the fabric in place.

2. Draw and cut out a heart shape with pinking shears from another piece of fabric and glue it in the middle of the lid. Glue rickrack around the edges.

3. Cut and glue lace around the edge of the box lid. Glue rickrack on top.

PAPER TREAT HOLDER
(construction paper)

1. Cut out a heart shape from a sheet of construction paper.

2. From another sheet of paper, cut a strip 2 inches wide. Draw a pencil line 1/2 inch from the edge of the strip. Make a fold on the pencil line. Open the fold and cut slits along the 1/2-inch section about 1/2 inch apart.

3. Spread glue along the clipped section and fit it around the bottom of the heart as shown. You may need to cut more than one strip to fit around the heart, depending on its size.

4. Decorate the outside of the box with paper hearts. Cut out and glue a heart with "Happy Valentine's Day" written on it. Fill the box with treats.

HEART GLASSES
(poster board, pink plastic wrap, self-adhesive stars)

1. Draw heart-shaped eyeglasses on pink poster board and cut them out along the dotted lines as shown in the diagram. (You can use a pair of old glasses to check the size.)

2. Cut and glue a piece of pink plastic wrap for the lenses. Add self-adhesive stars to decorate the front of the glasses.

3. Look through the glasses and see how everything looks "rosy."

GUESS WHO?
(construction paper, photograph)

1. Cut a square piece of construction paper. With a ruler, measure to find the center of each side of the square and draw a dot. Draw a straight line from one dot to the next as shown. Fold each corner into the center of the square.

2. Keeping the corners folded, write "Guess Who Loves You?" One word goes on each flap.

3. Open the flaps and glue a photograph of yourself in the center square. Write "I do!" under your picture.

4. Draw heart decorations around your photograph.

VALENTINE BOOKMARK
(paper doily, construction paper, clear self-adhesive paper, rickrack, yarn)

1. Cut small designs from a paper doily. Cut small hearts and arrows from construction paper.

2. Cut two identical shapes from clear self-adhesive paper for the bookmark. Carefully remove the backing from one bookmark shape, with the sticky side facing up. Press the hearts, arrows, and paper doily designs on the self-adhesive paper.

3. Place a strip of rickrack around the edge of the self-adhesive paper. Carefully remove the backing from the second bookmark shape. Place it on top of the first one, covering the cutout designs.

4. Punch a hole at one end of the bookmark and tie a piece of yarn through it.

PLASTIC HEART NECKLACE
(large clear plastic lid, nail polish, yarn)

1. Draw and cut out a heart shape from the center of a large clear plastic lid. Punch a hole at the top of the heart.

2. Paint a design on the heart with nail polish. You may want to let it dry, then put on another coat of polish.

3. Cut a piece of yarn long enough to fit over your head as a necklace. Thread the yarn through the hole and tie a knot.

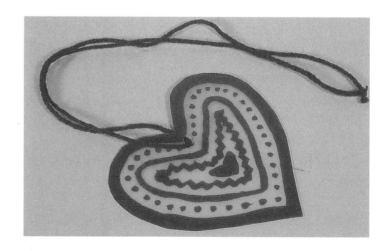

VALENTINE DOGGIE TREATS
(construction paper, two paper plates, yarn, dog biscuits)

1. Cut two heart shapes from construction paper, one larger than the other, and glue them together. Write a dog's name on the heart.

2. Cut away a small section of one paper plate as shown. Place the cut paper plate and a second paper plate face-to-face, making a pocket. Staple around the edges of the plates with the heart tucked in between them.

3. Glue on ears, eyes, eyelashes, a nose, and whiskers cut from construction paper. Punch two holes at the top and tie a piece of yarn for a hanger.

4. Place a few dog biscuits inside the pocket.

SACHET VALENTINE
(construction paper, paper doily, small white envelope, stickers, scented bath powder)

1. Cut a red paper heart and a white paper-doily heart the same size. Glue the paper doily heart on top of the red paper heart. Glue the heart to the front of a small white envelope.

2. Add cutout paper hearts and stickers to decorate the front of the envelope.

3. *Ask an adult* for some scented bath powder to put in the envelope. Seal the envelope and tape if necessary.

FROG HAS A MESSAGE
(construction paper, tracing paper, yarn, moveable plastic eyes)

1. Draw and cut out two frog shapes from green construction paper. Add details with markers from the mouth up on one frog and from the mouth down on the other frog.

2. Cut out the head and mouth of the first frog. Glue this shape on top of the second frog without gluing the mouth down. Fold the mouth open. Trace around the mouth shape on a piece of tracing paper and cut it out. Cut the same mouth shape from red paper and glue it inside the frog's mouth.

3. Draw and cut out a small white heart. Draw a fly on it with the message "You're a great catch!" Glue one end of a piece of yarn to the heart and the other end inside the frog's mouth so the heart hangs just below the mouth.

4. Glue moveable plastic eyes on the frog.

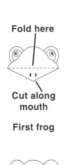

Fold here

Cut along mouth

First frog

Glue head here

Second frog

HEART HOT PAD
(waxed paper, twenty ice-cream sticks, felt)

1. Cover your work area with a sheet of waxed paper. Place ten ice-cream sticks next to each other with their sides touching. Squeeze glue on top.

2. Gently place the other ten ice-cream sticks in the glue crosswise on top of the first ten ice-cream sticks. Let dry.

3. Cut and glue a red felt heart in the center. Remove the hot pad from the waxed paper when dry.

HEART BANGLE BRACELET
(old newspaper, plastic ribbon ring, acrylic paint, nail polish)

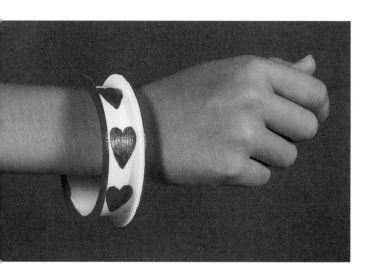

1. Cover your work area with old newspaper. Paint the outside of an empty plastic ribbon ring with two coats of white acrylic paint, letting the first coat dry before applying the second one.

2. Carefully paint two coats of red nail polish on one outside rim, letting the first coat of polish dry before applying the second. Do the same to the rim on the opposite side.

3. Paint small hearts on the flat area of the ribbon ring. Let dry.

PLEATED VALENTINE
(construction paper)

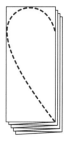

1. Fold a sheet of red construction paper into eight accordion pleats.

2. On the top draw a half-heart shape, making sure the outline touches the left and right edges of the folded paper. Cut around the outline, but leave the right edge and a small area that touches the left side uncut.

3. Open the folded paper. It will form four hearts. Write a message on them and re-pleat. Give the folded valentine to a friend.

PENNANT MESSAGE
(felt, wooden dowel, construction paper)

1. Cut a pennant shape from felt. Glue one end of the pennant around a wooden dowel. Let dry.

2. Decorate the pennant with sports designs cut from construction paper.

3. Draw and cut out a paper megaphone and write the message "You are a good sport, Valentine!" Glue it to the pennant.

RAIN-OR-SHINE MOUSE
(bathroom tissue tube, cardboard, felt, paper plate, large-eyed needle, chenille stick, paper)

1. Place the end of a bathroom tissue tube on cardboard and trace two circles. Cut out the cardboard circles and glue one to each end of the tube. Cover the tube with glue and brown felt for the body of the mouse.

2. To make the head, cut a small paper plate in half. Roll it into a cone shape and tape it on the inside. Glue it to one end of the body and let dry.

3. Poke holes through the snout with a large-eyed needle and push pieces of chenille stick through the holes for whiskers. Draw on a mouth and eyes. Cut and glue on felt ears.

4. Draw and cut out an umbrella shape from a paper plate. Write "Rain or shine be my Valentine" on the umbrella. Bend and tape a chenille stick for the handle.

5. Cut out four foot shapes from felt. Glue them to the body. Glue a red paper heart to one foot and the umbrella to the opposite foot. Cut a felt tail and glue it to the body.

HAT STAND
(scrap wallpaper, round oatmeal container, ribbon, lace, construction paper)

1. Tape or glue a section of scrap wallpaper around a round oatmeal container.

2. Glue ribbon and lace around the bottom and top of the container for decoration. Add cut-paper hearts.

3. Place your valentine hat on top.

WREATH OF HEARTS
(large brown paper bag, gift wrap, ribbon)

1. Remove the bottom from a large brown paper bag. Cut up one side of the bag, making a large sheet of paper.

2. Measure 2 1/2 inches up along the longest edge and draw a line. Cut out the strip. Measure and cut another strip. Glue the two strips together, making a strip that measures 36 inches long by 2 1/2 inches wide.

3. Crush and twist the strip tightly so it looks like a rope. Shape the strip into a circle that is 3 inches across, wrapping the remainder of the strip around the circle. Staple the ends together.

4. Glue hearts cut from gift wrap onto the wreath. Add a ribbon bow.

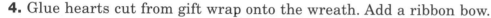

POCKET VALENTINE
(construction paper, yarn)

1. Fold a rectangle of construction paper in half. With the fold at the bottom, fold down the top front of the paper and cut it to look like a pocket flap. Glue the flap in place. Glue the sides together to form a pocket. Decorate with cut-paper shapes.

2. Cut out a paper heart and write a message on it. Punch a small hole near the top and tie a piece of yarn through the hole.

3. Tuck the heart into the pocket with the yarn hanging out.

BLUE RIBBON VALENTINE
(felt, gift wrap, fabric, plastic cap)

1. Cut out a circle from blue felt, making a decorative edge. Cut two strips of felt for the tails and glue them to the back of the circle.

2. Draw and cut out a circle from gift wrap. Glue it in the center on the front of the felt circle. Cut and glue a small circle of fabric on top.

3. Cover the top of a plastic cap with gift wrap. Cut out a fabric heart and glue it on top of the gift wrap.

4. Glue the plastic cap in the center of the circle.

WINDOW FLOWER HEART
(clear self-adhesive paper, tissue paper, cardboard, chenille stick)

1. Cut two identical heart shapes from clear self-adhesive paper. Carefully cut out tissue-paper flowers and leaves.

2. *Ask an adult to help you* peel the backing from one heart. Place the heart with the sticky side up on a cardboard work surface. Use two small pieces of tape to secure the heart to the cardboard so it won't move.

3. Gently place the cutout flowers and leaves on the sticky surface, covering the heart. Peel the backing from the second heart and place it on top, sealing the tissue flowers inside. Remove the tape.

4. Poke a hole at the center of the top of the heart. Wrap one end of a chenille stick through the hole for a hanger.

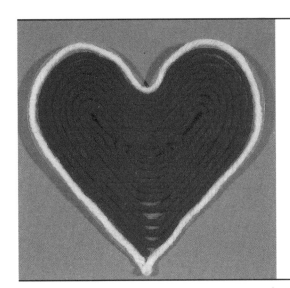

YARN-HEART COASTER
(clear plastic lid, waxed paper, fabric glue, yarn)

1. Cut a heart shape from a clear plastic lid. Place the heart on a piece of waxed paper.

2. Squeeze fabric glue around the outer edge of the heart. Press a long piece of white yarn into the glue outline.

3. Switch to red yarn and continue to add more glue and more yarn, working toward the center of the plastic heart. Let dry overnight.

SWEETHEART FAN
(five ice-cream sticks, ribbon, construction paper)

1. Place five ice-cream sticks in a fan shape. Glue the sticks, stacking one on top of the other at the bottom where they meet. Let dry.

2. Make a ribbon bow, and glue it to the bottom of the fan. Cut out two paper hearts. Write a message on the hearts and glue them to the middle of the fan.

3. Draw and cut out small hearts and glue them to the tips of the sticks. Add pieces of ribbon below the small hearts.

STAND-UP VALENTINE
(construction paper)

1. Cut two identical squares of construction paper, one red and one white. Cut the white square into a heart shape and draw a face on it.

2. Cut a strip of red paper the same length as the red square. Place the heart face down on the red square with about 2 inches of the top of the heart overlapping the edge of the square.

3. Glue one end of the strip to the red square and the other end to the back of the heart.

4. When the glue is dry, bend the strip back in the middle without creasing it, so that the heart stands up on the red square.

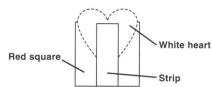

Red square — White heart — Strip

CUPID MAGNET
(red paper plates, white paper plate, moveable plastic eyes, magnetic strip)

1. Cut six hearts of various sizes from red paper plates. Use the largest heart for the body, the next largest for the head, and four small hearts for the arms and legs. Glue the hearts together to form Cupid.

2. To make wings, cut two small triangular sections from a white paper plate. Glue them to the back of Cupid.

3. Add moveable plastic eyes. Cut a nose and mouth from a white paper plate and glue in place.

4. Glue a magnetic strip to Cupid's back.

LACY VALENTINE
(paper doily, construction paper, white paper, needle and embroidery floss)

1. Glue a white paper doily on top of a sheet of red construction paper. When dry, cut out a large heart.

2. Cut out a small heart from white paper and glue it in the center of the large heart. Write a message on it.

3. Thread a large embroidery needle with six strands of red embroidery floss. Use a running stitch to stitch around the edges of both the small and large heart.

Running stitch

VALENTINE FISH MOBILE
(plastic milk jug, construction paper, yarn)

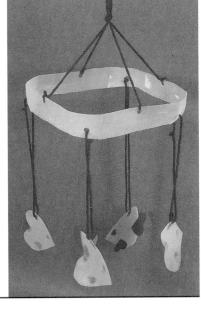

1. Cut four heart shapes from the sides of a clean plastic milk jug for the fish bodies.

2. Cut out three red paper hearts for each fish. Use one large heart for the tail, one medium heart for a fin, and one small heart for an eye. Glue the paper hearts on the fish. Punch a hole in the top of each fish.

3. Draw and cut a ring from the bottom of the plastic jug. Punch a hole in the center of each side section of the ring near the top. Cut four strands of yarn and tie one to each hole. Then tie the strands together at the top to form a hanger.

4. Punch four holes, one at each corner of the ring. Cut four strands of yarn. Tie one fish to each corner hole in the ring.

LICORICE HOLDER
(large frozen-juice container, fabric, rubber band, ribbon)

1. Turn a large frozen-juice container upside down. Place a piece of fabric over it, letting the fabric cover the container and leaving a few extra inches.

2. Pick up the upside-down container and gather the fabric near the opening. Place a rubber band around the gathered fabric about an inch below the top.

3. Tie a ribbon around the fabric-covered container on top of the rubber band. Use scissors to trim the fabric evenly above the container.

4. Place red licorice into the holder.

SPYGLASS VALENTINE
(paper towel tube, poster paint, paper)

1. Cover a paper towel tube with red poster paint and let dry.

2. Cut a paper label and write "Look Through This End." Add an arrow pointing to the left. Glue the label on the left end of the tube.

3. Cut out two paper hearts. On one write "To:" and add the name of the person who will receive the valentine. On the other heart write "From:" and add your name. Glue the hearts on the right end of the tube.

4. Place the right end of the tube on a piece of paper and trace around it, making a circle. Inside the circle draw a heart and write "Be Mine." Cut out the circle, making it about 1/2 inch larger, and place it over the opening of the right end of the tube with the writing on the inside. Glue the edges of the circle to the outside of the tube.

5. Hold the tube up to the light and look through the opened end. You should be able to read the message.

VALENTINE PUZZLE RACE
(corrugated cardboard, paint, permanent marker)

1. Draw and cut out two identical large corrugated cardboard hearts. Cover one heart with red paint and the other one with pink paint. Let them dry and add another coat of paint to each if needed.

2. Using a permanent marker, write "Be Mine, Valentine!" on one heart. On the other heart write "Don't Break My Heart!" *Ask an adult to help you* cut each heart into pieces.

To play: Starting at the same time, each player must try to put his or her heart puzzle together. The first player to complete the puzzle wins.

PLASTIC-FOAM NECKLACE
(plastic-foam trays, needle and thread)

1. Use a paper punch to punch dots from white and pink plastic-foam trays. Draw and cut out a heart shape from a white tray and decorate it with dots.

2. Cut a piece of heavy thread long enough to go over your head easily. Thread a sewing needle with the heavy thread, but do not tie a knot in the end. Make a necklace chain by sewing through the center of each white dot and sewing sideways through the pink ones.

3. Be sure to leave long ends of thread at each end of the chain. Sew the ends of the chain to the heart.

VALENTINE INVITATION
(construction paper, glitter)

1. Fold a piece of white construction paper in half for the card. Cut out a red paper heart and gently tear it down the middle. Glue it to the front of the card, leaving a little space between the torn edges.

2. Outline the edges of the heart and make a border on the card with glue and glitter.

3. Inside the invitation write "My heart will break
   If you don't say
   You'll come to my party
   For Valentine's Day."

Add your name, address, phone number, and date and time of the party.

ALPHABET VALENTINES
(construction paper)

The secret to these valentines is that the first word of the message is the shape of the valentine itself.

1. Cut out a large letter from construction paper. Write a message to go with the letter. For example, cut the letter *B* from red paper. Write the words "My Valentine." Your real message is "Be My Valentine."

2. You can also make "words" with the letters *C, A, O, G,* and *U.* Think of others and write a message to go with each letter.

FLOWER BOUQUET
(food container with plastic lid, construction paper,
plastic-foam egg carton, chenille sticks)

1. Cover a clean food container and its plastic lid with construction paper. Decorate the sides with cut-paper hearts.

2. From a plastic-foam egg carton, cut cup sections in flower shapes. Cut and glue paper hearts on the flowers.

3. With a pencil, poke a small hole in the bottom of each flower. Insert a long chenille stick through the hole for a stem.

4. Cut out paper hearts for leaves. Glue a small plastic-foam heart, cut from the lid of the egg carton, in the center of each paper-heart leaf. Glue the leaves on the stems and let dry.

5. *Ask an adult to help you* poke a hole in the center of the plastic lid. Place the flowers through the hole to make them stand up.

CAT TOY
(felt, paper, permanent markers, fabric glue, catnip)

1. Cut out two felt hearts the same size.

2. From paper, draw and cut out a cat's head that will fit on the heart shape. Pin the paper cat on a piece of felt and cut it out. Use fabric glue to attach the cat's head to one of the hearts. Add features with permanent markers.

3. Squeeze fabric glue around the edge of the plain heart. Cut out a felt tail and place it just inside the edge of the heart. Sprinkle a little catnip in the center of the heart.

4. Place the heart with the cat's head on top, pressing the edges together. Let dry.

MANY HEARTS VALENTINE
(construction paper, yarn)

1. Cut a 9-by-18-inch rectangle from red construction paper. Fold it in half, making a 9-inch square.

2. Cut a sheet of white paper into an 8-inch square. Fold the square in half. Cut out six small hearts as shown in Section 1. Open the paper and fold it in half the other way. Cut out six hearts as shown in Section 2.

3. Open the paper and fold it in half diagonally. Cut out eight hearts as shown in Section 3. Open the paper and fold it in half diagonally the other way. Cut out eight hearts as shown in Section 4.

4. Open the paper and glue it to the center of the 9-inch red square. Punch two holes close to the fold. Thread a piece of yarn through the holes and tie a bow. Write a message inside the card.

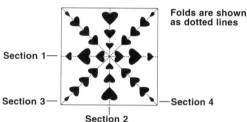

Folds are shown as dotted lines

Section 1 — Section 2 — Section 3 — Section 4

HEART RING
(lightweight cardboard, construction paper, chenille stick, beads)

1. Draw and cut out a small heart shape from lightweight cardboard. Trace around it twice on red construction paper. Cut out the hearts and glue one to each side of the cardboard heart.

2. Cut and glue a red chenille stick heart to the back of the cardboard heart.

3. Cut a piece of chenille stick to go around your finger. Glue it to the back of the cardboard heart. Let dry.

4. Put the ring on your finger and twist the ends of the chenille stick together. Remove the ring. Trim off any extra ends. Place the ring upright. Glue small beads around the edge of the heart. Let dry.

SECRET MESSAGE VALENTINE
(construction paper)

1. Fold a sheet of red construction paper in half the long way. Draw and cut three hearts almost all the way out, leaving about an inch at the top of each heart to hold the paper together.

2. Draw and cut out heart shapes along the sides as shown.

3. Glue the red paper on a sheet of white paper, attaching everything but the center row of hearts. Lift each of the center hearts and write your message on the white sheet underneath.

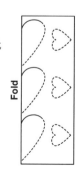

BIRDSEED MOBILE
(waxed paper, plastic lids, ribbon, peanut butter, birdseed)

1. Cover your work surface with waxed paper. Cut out hearts from plastic lids. Punch a hole at the top and bottom of each heart.

2. Tie the hearts together with pieces of ribbon.

3. Spread one side of each heart with peanut butter. Then press each side in birdseed. Turn the hearts over and cover the other side.

4. Hang the mobile outside to give the birds a valentine treat.

LOLLIPOP PLACE CARD
(construction paper, flat lollipop, gumdrop)

1. Cut out a heart shape from construction paper for each place card. Make two slits in each one and insert a cut-paper arrow with a guest's name printed on it.

2. Glue the heart to the wrapper of a flat lollipop and stand it upright in a large gumdrop.

DESK DECORATION
(construction paper)

1. Use a sheet of red construction paper that measures 12 inches by 18 inches. Place it lengthwise in front of you. Draw vertical lines 10 1/2 inches long and 2 1/2 inches apart. With scissors, cut along the lines, making slits. Do not cut to the edges of the paper.

2. Cut strips of white paper, 2 1/2 inches wide by 18 inches in length. Weave them in and out of the slits on the red paper, making a checkerboard. Glue the ends of the strips.

3. Cut red paper hearts and glue them to the white squares.

CLOUD CUPID CARD
(construction paper, cotton balls)

1. Fold a sheet of light blue construction paper in half to form a card.

2. Draw and cut out Cupid from red paper. Add eyes and a mouth with a marker. Cut out a yellow paper sun.

3. Glue cotton balls on the card in a cloud shape. Add the sun and Cupid.

4. Write "Valentine . . ." on the front of the card. On the inside write "I'm floating on a cloud whenever you're around!"

VALENTINE COLLAGE
(lightweight cardboard, valentine cards, construction paper, yarn)

1. Cut out a large heart from a piece of lightweight cardboard. Glue some valentine cards on the heart.

2. Draw and cut out hearts of various colors and sizes from paper. Glue them onto the heart, overlapping the cards.

3. Squeeze glue around the edge of the large heart. Press a piece of yarn into the glue. Add a yarn bow. Let dry.

4. Tape or glue a loop of yarn to the back for a hanger.

GIFT OF FLOWERS
(construction paper, paper doily, ribbon)

1. Cut and glue a circle of red construction paper in the center of a round white paper doily.

2. Draw and cut stems and leaves from green paper. Cut out red and pink paper tulips. Glue the flowers to the stems. Then glue the flowers and leaves around the paper doily and let dry.

3. Fold the circle in half and glue it together. Punch a hole at the top. Thread a piece of ribbon through the hole and tie a pretty bow.

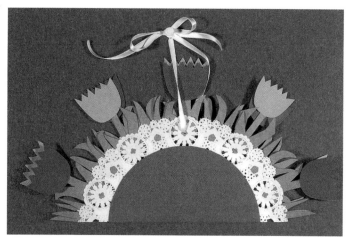

INCOMING MAIL

(shoe box, cardboard, one-pound coffee can with plastic lid, construction paper)

1. With the lid off, trace around one end of a shoe box on cardboard. Draw 2-inch flaps on the two long sides of the rectangle shape and cut it out. Fold up the flaps along the pencil lines. Staple this to one end of the shoe box with the flaps up.

2. Place the coffee can between the flaps. Tape the flaps to the can. Tape the ends of the can to the box. Cut off one end of the shoe-box lid. Close the shoe box and tape it shut.

3. *Ask an adult to help you* cut a mail slot in the shoe box. Cover the mailbox with construction paper. Decorate the mailbox with cut-paper hearts.

4. To remove valentines from the mailbox, cut a door in the back of the box.

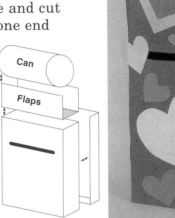

CLAY VALENTINE

(construction paper, greeting card box with clear acetate top, clay)

1. Cut and glue construction paper around the outside and inside of the bottom of a greeting card box that has a clear acetate top.

2. Press and mold clay inside the card box to look like a picture frame. Mold hearts of a different-colored clay and place them on the corners of the clay frame. Add a large clay heart in the center.

3. Roll thin strips of clay and form letters to spell the message "Be Mine." Add them to the large heart.

4. Place the clear acetate top on the box.

VALENTINE NOISEMAKER

(aluminum pie pans, yarn, dried beans, construction paper)

1. Place two small aluminum pie pans facing each other, rim to rim. Hold the rims together and, with a paper punch, punch holes around the edges so the holes line up.

2. Cut short pieces of yarn. Tie one piece of yarn through each set of holes, joining the two rims together. Before tying the last set of holes together, place a few dried beans between the pans. Tie pieces of yarn near each knot so they dangle around the noisemaker.

3. Cut paper hearts from construction paper and glue onto the pans.

Baskets and More

Give your gifts in a special way.

WRAPPING PAPER
(old newspaper, poster paper, poster board,
tempera paint, paper plate, old toothbrush)

1. *Ask an adult to help you* select a work area and cover it with old newspaper. Cut a section from a roll of poster paper. Tape each corner to the newspaper to hold it in place.

2. Draw and cut out hearts from poster board. Place the hearts onto the poster paper, holding them in place with small pieces of rolled tape on the backs.

3. Squeeze different colors of tempera paint onto a paper plate. Carefully dip the bristles of an old toothbrush in one color. Hold the brush in one hand close to the poster paper near a taped-on heart. With the other hand, run your finger sideways over the bristles, spattering paint onto the poster paper.

4. Continue to spatter paint lightly onto the poster paper until it is covered. Let dry. Carefully remove the taped-on hearts.

HEART BASKET
(eight ice-cream sticks, watercolor paint, construction paper, plastic berry basket)

1. Paint eight ice-cream sticks with green watercolor paint and let dry.

2. Cut out eight heart shapes from pink and red construction paper. Glue them to the ends of the sticks. Add smaller hearts to the centers of the larger hearts.

3. Weave the ice-cream sticks through the sides of a plastic berry basket. Put candy inside.

GIFT BAG
(small paper bag, poster paint, paper doily, paper, ribbon)

1. Cover the outside of a small paper bag with pink poster paint and let dry. Cut out a heart shape from a white paper doily. Glue it to the center of the bag.

2. Cut small red paper hearts and glue them along the bottom of the bag.

3. Holding the bag closed, punch a hole through all layers at the top. Open the bag and place a gift inside. Close the bag, thread a piece of red ribbon through the holes, and tie a bow.

WOVEN HEART BASKET
(construction paper)

1. Fold a sheet of white and a sheet of red construction paper in half the long way. Draw and cut out a large U-shape from each sheet of paper, and cut three slits as shown in the diagram.

2. Weave the four looplike sections as shown in the diagram. The first left white loop is inserted into the first red right loop, then over the second red loop. The second white loop is slipped over the first red loop and inserted into the second red loop.

3. Continue to weave until all the sections are woven together. Slide them together to fit snugly. Glue a paper handle onto the basket and fill with a snack.

GIFT BOX
(small gift box, poster paint, construction paper, yarn)

1. Draw and cut out a heart shape from the lid of a small gift box. Cover the lid with poster paint and let dry.

2. Turn the lid over on a piece of white construction paper and trace around the cutout heart shape. Draw red heart outlines on the white heart.

3. Cut out and glue a small red paper heart on top of a pink paper heart. Glue a ring of paper to the back of the hearts and glue them to the center of the white heart. Glue the white heart in the cutout center of the box lid. Glue yarn around the heart and the edge of the box.

4. Draw and cut out paper letters that spell "Be Mine" and glue them to the lid.

MINI CANDY BASKET
(cardboard egg carton, poster paint, construction paper)

1. Cut a cup section from a cardboard egg carton for the basket. Cover it with white poster paint and let dry.

2. Draw and cut out four red paper heart shapes. Cut out the centers. Glue pink paper on one side of the red hearts so the pink paper shows through on the other side.

3. Glue the hearts around the basket. Cut and glue a paper handle inside the basket on opposite sides. Fill the basket with candies.

MATERIAL INDEX

ALUMINUM PIE PANS:
Valentine Noisemaker 59

BERRY BASKET:
Heart Basket 60
Just for Mom 30
Sweetheart Basket 6

BOX OF FACIAL TISSUES:
Holiday Tissue Box 43

BUTTONS:
Button Card 41

CALENDAR:
Heart Toss Game 20

CARDBOARD:
Valentine Puzzle Race 54

CARDBOARD BOXES:
Fabric Jewelry Box 45
Gift Box 61
Incoming Mail 59
Sweetheart House 24
Valentine Carrier 12
Valentine Mobile 5

CARDBOARD CONTAINERS:
Cupid's Arrow Game 37
Hat Stand 49
Licorice Holder 53

**CARDBOARD EGG
CARTONS:**
"Bee" Mine, Valentine 8
Egg Carton Jewelry Box 20
Mini Candy Basket 61

**CARDBOARD SALT AND
PEPPER SHAKERS:**
Salt and Pepper Shakers 35

CARDBOARD TUBES:
Rain-or-Shine Mouse 49
Spyglass Valentine 53
Surprise Valentine Tube 8
Valentine Ringtoss 29

CARDS:
Valentine Collage 58

CATALOG:
Secret Hearts Valentine 28

CHENILLE STICKS:
Chenille-Stick Doll 25
Heart Ring 56

CLAY:
Clay Valentine 59

CONSTRUCTION PAPER:
Alphabet Valentines 55
Caterpillar Valentine 44
Desk Decoration 57
Frog Has a Message 47
Guess Who? 46
Heart-in-Hand Valentines . . 28
Mail-Truck Holder 3
Many Hearts Valentine 56
Necklace of Hearts 40
Needle-Punched Card 43
Paper-Doll Valentine 18
Paper Treat Holder 45
Peanut Valentine 9
Piggy-Bank Valentine Card . . 19
Pleated Valentine 48
Pocket Valentine 50
Secret Message Valentine . . . 56
Stand-Up Valentine 52
Valentine Bookmark Card . . . 38
Valentine Crown 24
Valentine Garland 25
Valentine Invitation 54
Valentine Mobile 39
Valentine Mouse Bookmark . 18
Valentine Mouse Card 4
Worm Card 6
Woven Heart Basket 61

COTTON BALLS:
Cloud Cupid Card 58
Valentine Rabbit 21

CREPE PAPER:
Fluttering Heart 16

ENVELOPE:
Sachet Valentine 47

FABRIC:
Book of Hearts 29
Doorknob Decoration 27
Fabric Flowers 23
Fabric-Heart Place Mat 34
Fabric Photo Frame 39
Heart Hotpad 17
"Knots About You" Wreath . . . 4
Patchwork Card 10

FELT:
Blue Ribbon Valentine 50
Cat Toy 55
Felt-Heart Centerpiece 35
Heart Pin Gift and Card 15
Lacy Bag. 13
Pennant Message 49
Sewing Needle Case 6
Sweet-Smelling Valentines . . . 5
Valentine's Day Banner 36

FLOWERPOT:
Planter of Love 9
Potted Packet 44

GLASS BOTTLE:
Candle Holder 41

GLITTER:
Glittering Heart Pin 26

GLOVES:
Flowered Garden Gloves 33

ICE-CREAM STICKS:
Heart Hot Pad 48
Heart Ice-Cream-Stick Holder . . 39
Sentimental Slate 11
Sweetheart Fan 51

INDEX CARDS:
Valentine Recipe Cards 27

KNITTED HAT AND GLOVES:
Hat and Glove Set 32

LOLLIPOPS:
Lollipop Place Card 57
Lollipops for Sister 30

MAGAZINES:
Meet the Best Grandpa 31
Valentines from the Garden . . . 14

METAL BARRETTE BASE:
Hair Clip 43

MILK CARTONS:
Heart Napkin Holder 35
Heart Nut Box 15

PAINT STIR STICK:
Spinning Hearts 7

PAPER:
Punched-Card Valentines . . . 40
Rainbow Heart Hanger 14
Roll-a-Heart Valentine 12
Signed, "I Love You" 16
Twirling Heart Mobile 12

PAPER BAGS:
Gift Bag 60
Paper-Bag Holder 3
Valentine Kite 40
Wreath of Hearts 50

PAPER CUP:
Heart Candy Box 22

PAPER DOILIES:
Doily Basket 36
Gift of Flowers 58
Heart Notepad 22
Lacy Valentine 52
Valentine Wand 9

PAPER PLATES:
Big Valentine Hug, A 26
Cupid Magnet 52
Paper-Plate Holder 3
Valentine Doggie Treats 47
Valentine Ring 7

PAPER TABLECLOTH:
Personalized Tablecloth 34

PENCIL:
Pencil Valentine 24

PICTURE FRAME:
Three-D Framed Flowers . . . 42

PINECONES:
Heart-Shaped
  Pinecone Wreath 28

PLASTIC BOTTLES:
Plastic Birdhouse 27
Sun Catcher for Grandma . . . 31
Valentine Candy Holder 17
Valentine Dancer 13
Yarn Vase 38

PLASTIC CAPS:
Hearts Game, The 11
Tabletop Valentines 34
Valentine Tic-Tac-Toe 7

PLASTIC CONTAINER:
Pet Dish 17

PLASTIC CUP:
Red Bird 37

PLASTIC-FOAM CUPS:
Cupid Pop-up 29
Valentine Bracelets 8

**PLASTIC-FOAM
EGG CARTON:**
Flower Bouquet 55

PLASTIC-FOAM "PEANUTS":
Dove Door Decoration 10

PLASTIC-FOAM TRAYS:
Cityscape for Dad 30
Heart Bell 44
Plastic-Foam Necklace 54
Sweetheart Photo Frame 21

PLASTIC JUG:
Valentine Fish Mobile 53

PLASTIC LIDS:
Birdseed Mobile 57
Heart Coasters 26
Key Chain 5
Plastic Heart Necklace 46
Puffy Heart Magnet 41
Yarn-Heart Coaster 51

PLASTIC RIBBON RING:
Heart Bangle Bracelet 48

PLASTIC WRAP:
Heart Glasses 45

POSTER BOARD:
Bat for Brother, A 31
Butterfly Hearts 36
Sweetheart Hat 4
Three-D Valentine Card 22
Valentine Portrait 19

POSTER PAINT:
Tree of Sweethearts 19

POSTER PAPER:
Wrapping Paper 60

POTATO:
Potato Print Stationery 23

ROCK:
Rock Paperweight 14

SELF-ADHESIVE PAPER:
Valentine Bookmark 46
Window Flower Heart 51

**SELF-ADHESIVE
REINFORCEMENT RINGS:**
Lacy Ring Valentine 20

SHIRT:
Heart Print Shirt 33

SHOESTRING:
Bolo Tie 33

SNEAKERS:
Valentine Footwear 32

SOCKS:
Sweetheart Socks 32
Valentine Pals 11

**SPRING-TYPE
CLOTHESPINS:**
Heart Snack Holders 42
Valentine Butterfly Message . 16

THREAD SPOOL:
Four-Leaf Clover Valentine . . 13

TISSUE PAPER:
Tissue Flowers 15
Valentine Design 25
Valentine Sequin Pin 38

TOOTHPICKS:
Three-Sided Heart Picks 21

WIRE CLOTHES HANGER:
Valentine Mobile, A 23

YARN:
Doorknob Surprise 42
"I Love You" Bookmark 10
Valentine Necklace 18
Yarn Valentine 37